CW01647739

HUGE DEAL

A BROTHER'S BEST FRIENDS REVERSE HAREM ROMANCE

STEPHANIE BROTHER

HUGE DEAL Copyright © 2023
STEPHANIE BROTHER

All Rights Reserved. This book or any portion thereof may not be reproduced or used in any manner whatsoever without the express permission of the publisher except for the use of brief quotations in a book review.

This book is a work of fiction. Any resemblance to persons, living or dead, or places, events or locations is purely coincidental. The characters are all productions of the author's imagination.

Please note that this work is intended only for adults over the age of 18 and all characters represented as 18 or over.

Chapter divider by Vecteezy.com

ISBN: 9781915436061

1

KAIN

"I need you to do me a favor," Travis says. The phone line crackles and then it seems to go dead.

"Travis. You there?" I twist to glance at the screen, checking to see if the call has disconnected, but the timer continues to tick. I expected the phone connection from Germany to be better than this.

"Can you hear me?" Travis yells.

"Yeah, bro," I say. "What favor?"

"I need you to go over to my house and clear the dirty magazines out of my closet. Mom just told me she's going to decorate my room while I'm gone, and I don't want her to find them."

I snort, shaking my head. "You seriously give a fuck about your mom finding that? She knows you're not a kid anymore. Right? And you're not a virgin, for fuck's sake." I pause for theatrical effect. "You aren't a virgin anymore, are you?"

"Fuck off," Travis laughs. The line crackles again, distorting the sound of his amusement. "Just tell her I've asked you guys to help her move my stuff so that she doesn't do her back in again. She'll be grateful. And then, while you're packing and shifting boxes, you can bag up the unmentionables."

"And do what with them?" I flop onto the couch, tired at just the thought of carrying out Travis's instructions. Even though it's going to be a ball ache, I won't say no. I'd never say no to my best friend.

"Keep them safe for when I get back. There's some classic stuff there."

"Classic?" My mind conjures nineteen-seventies style bushes, but before Travis can elaborate, I cut him off. "In fact, don't tell me. I don't want to know."

"And say hi to Gabriella from me."

Gabriella. If talking about classic porn had my mind drifting to filthy places, the mention of Travis's sister might as well send me to hell. Long golden hair, curves for days, and legs that seem to stretch up to the heavens. Her mom named her after an angel, and she seems to have taken that form on earth. If she wasn't Travis's sister, I'd be all over her like a rash. We all would be. Blake and Dalton have the same taste as me in women and we've had more than one conversation about how hot she is.

"You want me to say hi to your sister? Don't you speak to her?"

"I'm working so damned hard right now. It's hard to find time to take a dump."

I snort, as images I'd rather weren't taking residence in my head do so anyway. "I'll tell her."

My older brother, Dalton, lumbers into the room, slumping into the chair opposite me. He deflates in front of me, letting all his muscles relax, the exhaustion of a hard day's work pouring off him. Dad keeps him busy at whatever construction site is their current focus. He's priming him to take over the family business. I guess I should be grateful that he wants to because me and Blake have absolutely no interest in it.

"I just want to let you know it hasn't passed unnoticed that you have time to call me about your porn collection, but no time to call your sister to say hi," I say, and laugh silently at Dalton's comically raised eyebrows.

"Don't give me shit, Kain. Just get over there before my mom goes foraging and can never look me in the eye again."

This time, when the line crackles, it disconnects, but it doesn't matter. Travis made it clear what I need to do to help.

"What was that about?" Dalton asks, stretching like a lazy cat. The latest tattoo our brother Blake inked for him comes into view as his shirt tugs over his bicep. It's a tiger, framed by a large, spiked plant. Awesome art, but I don't get the appeal of being permanently marked by something you might grow to hate in the future.

"Travis's mom is going to decorate his room while he's overseas, and he's worried about her finding his sketchy 'classic' porn collection." I say classic and make air quotes because I still don't know what it means.

"Seriously?" Dalton flops his arms by his sides and rolls his head on his neck.

"Seriously. And he wants us to help box up his other stuff and move it so that his mom doesn't hurt herself."

"When."

"ASAP," I say.

"Now?"

I nod at him and raise my eyebrows. "You've just exhaled enough breath to extinguish a forest fire and cracked every one of your vertebrae. You sure you're in a fit state to do anything?"

"Don't start again about who's fitter." Dalton rolls his eyes and I grab the cushion next to me and toss it at his head.

"I don't need to start again," I say. "Because it's me."

He flexes his big biceps and smirks. "You see this? It's built on real work, Kain. Not fancy push-ups while Coach tells you what a good boy you are."

"Fuck you." I toss another pillow in his direction and he catches it, hurling it back.

"Where's Blake?" I ask.

"Washing his hair," Dalton scoffs, as though he considers anything over two minutes under cold water with army regulation soap something only a girl would do. All that time he's spent on construction sites seems to have warped his brain.

"Go tell him we're needed next door. No time like the present."

"And what are you going to do?" Dalton asks, struggling to his feet.

"I'm going to search out a bag so we can smuggle all those filthy magazines out of that house."

"Good thinking. I'm sure Travis won't mind us taking a look." Dalton wiggles his eyebrows, widening his blue eyes comically.

"The prospect of jacking off to the same shit as my best mate isn't that appealing." Construction sites have ruined Dalton for good.

Blake is in the shower for another fifteen minutes, much to Dalton's amusement, and in that time, I root out a suitable bag and make us all sandwiches that better resemble doorsteps. My taste buds beg for a delicious hot meal. Anything involving meat and potatoes would hit the spot, but with four men in this house, culinary skills are in short supply.

We wolf down our makeshift meal and head next door before Dad arrives home and gets involved. It's a journey that I could take in my sleep. Every uneven paving stone is familiar, every overhanging plant comes with a happy childhood memory.

Travis's house has always been like a second home to us. Well, at least it was while Travis was living there. Since his company posted him to their headquarters in Berlin, things have felt different. It's not that Darleen, his mom, isn't friendly. It's more that our acceptable reason for going over isn't there anymore.

And I miss it.

The warmth of a home with a mom in it cannot be underestimated. Travis and I both lost parents, but his home is still just as inviting, whereas ours has turned into a man cave, and not a nice one.

The appeal of a home with Gabriella in it also can't be underestimated.

Her car is out front, so I know she's home. I glance up at the window to her room, wondering if she's watching us make our approach. Probably not. As far as I can tell, she's always just thought of us as her brother's annoying friends who take up too much space in the den and monopolize the TV.

Darleen is quick to answer our knock and draws us all in for warm hugs, ending with her hands on her hips and her chin tipped up to take us in. "You guys been rubbing fertilizer into your feet again? Surely you should have stopped growing by now."

"We're growing this way these days," Dalton says, flexing his bicep, and I roll my eyes. Seriously? He wants to show off to Travis's mom like he did when he was ten. Lame.

"Travis called us. He asked us to come round and clean out his room so that you can decorate."

"He did? That's so thoughtful of him to ask for your help. You go on up. I've already started packing boxes.

You can just carry on while I fix dinner. You'll stay, won't you?"

Before Blake and Dalton can jump in and say yes, I interject. "I'm afraid we can't," I say. "We just ate."

"Oh," Darleen says, touching her short blonde hair. "Maybe another time?"

"That would be awesome." It really would be. A chance to sit across from Gabriella and eat some of Darleen's delicious cooking. Awesome is frankly an understatement.

"Gabriella's up there," she says. "Say hi. She'll be happy to see you. The house has seemed so quiet since Travis left."

"We will," Blake says breezily, but I feel anything but. It's been weeks since I saw Gabriella for more than a fleeting moment, and I'm craving the sight of her like an addict.

We remove our shoes at the bottom of the stairs, following Darleen's rule, and make our way up to the top floor where Travis and Gabriella have rooms. Travis's door is open, but Gabby's is disappointingly shut. There's a bathroom between their rooms that we used to pretend was a portal to another universe, Planet Angel. We'd slide across the floor and crawl into Gabriella's room, and she'd scream at the unwelcome invasion. The memory makes me smile.

"Keep your voices down," I whisper. "She might be sleeping."

Dalton snorts as we enter the room we practically lived in when we were kids. "What do you want to do? Tiptoe into her room and kiss her awake like the prince from Sleeping Beauty."

"I'm trying to avoid being a douchebag," I say, scowling.

"Do you guys ever stop bitchin'?" Blake asks, rubbing

his latest tattoo. It's a pirate ship, leaning on a rough sea. Incredible art, but not for me.

I have my hand on the closet door when there's an agonized shout from Gabby's room, followed by the clatter of something hitting the hardwood floor. I don't even think about what I'm doing before I barrel through the door to the shared bathroom and burst into Gabriella's room, expecting to find her lying injured on the floor and in need of rescue.

Maybe I am channeling the rescuing prince today.

Instead, I find her lying on her bed, legs spread wide and pussy bared, panting as her magic wand vibrator spins out of control on the floor. Her glazed eyes lock onto mine, shock cutting through the aftermath of what I now realize was an orgasm, not a domestic accident. With her blonde hair spilling out over the pillows, she really looks like a fairy-tale princess. At least, one who's gotten to the end of the fairy tale and is seeking her happily ever after ending.

Blake and Dalton stumble into me from behind, and I'm almost propelled headfirst onto Gabby's bed, just as she finally snaps into action and jumps up, her skirt falling to cover her nakedness.

Shit. Shit. Shit.

Grabbing the vibrator, she stands before us like an avenging angel clutching an instrument of heavenly wrath. When she finds the switch, the low hum it was emitting stops immediately, and then the room is silent.

Silent except for my blood rushing in my ears and my heart hammering in my chest.

"GET OUT," she yells, her face redder than a tomato ripened in the summer sun. "GET OUT!"

I take a step back, treading on Blake's foot. When I turn, I find my two brothers stunned into an open-mouthed stupor. "You heard her. Get out."

I hook my arm into Dalton's and drag him back through the bathroom, turning to make sure Blake is following. He is, thank goodness.

The bathroom door slams on Gabby's side and locks.

And in the aftermath of that click, I stare at my brothers, not quite believing what has just happened. And definitely not believing what we just saw.

Gabriella Cross masturbating. I just saw the pussy of the girl I've been crushing on for years. And instead of being mortified for her, I want to close my eyes and think about that image to cement it into my brain forever. I've never wanted a photographic memory more than I do at this moment.

"Did you see that?" Dalton mutters, his shock still making him appear like a startled goldfish. He rubs the back of his neck, shaking his head.

"No, I ran in there with my eyes closed," I snort.

"We just heard Travis's little sister come," Blake says, chuckling devilishly.

"It sounded painful," Dalton muses.

"It's a fucking waste," I say. "A travesty. An injustice that such a gorgeous girl has to resort to battery operated pleasure."

Blake slumps onto Travis's bed, folding his arms behind his head. "Maybe you should offer her your cock, you know, as community service."

"Maybe you should shut your fucking mouth," I say.

"That's actually not a bad idea," Dalton says. "I think I will."

The murderous rage I feel thunder through me hits me off guard. "Like fuck you will," I hiss, as my body primes for violence.

"Maybe we all should," Blake muses. "I mean, that vibrator was some serious kit, and it's only early evening right now. The girl was too thirsty to wait until the cover of darkness. Aaaannnd…" He drags out the word as though he wants to emphasize that he's about to make his most important point. "…we've all been crushing on Gabriella Cross since before we grew hair on our balls. It's the only solution that would be fair and equitable."

"Do you hear yourself?" I snarl. "You're talking about Travis's little sister, a girl we grew up with, a girl we should respect."

"Oh, I respect her. I respect her need for pleasure that doesn't come from a hard, plastic object. I respect her enough to lend her the use of my most prized body part."

"Not your brain, then," Dalton mutters. The smile that tugs at the corner of his lips makes me want to punch him, but at least he's not taking Blake's suggestion seriously.

Blake fixes him with a knowing stare. "You've been beating your meat over Gabby for years."

I swivel to fix dagger-eyes at a suddenly shifty-looking Dalton, who shrugs his shoulders. "What can I say? I'm a man with eyes and a cock. And a busy right hand."

"And you." Blake raises his eyebrows, nodding in my direction. I don't like how exposed it makes me feel. They're talking about Gabby like she's a piece of meat, but I've always wanted more from her than just her sweet tits and rounded ass. I've wanted a chance to make her smile. I've wanted to make her my girl.

"This isn't right," I say.

"Of course it is." Blake swivels his legs off the bed and stretches his arms above his head. "If we don't, some other asshole out there will. Watching some other asshole take the place we could occupy would eat me from the inside out. We can make her a deal. A strictly no-strings offer that will result in her ultimate satisfaction. Just until she finds a decent man to have a loving relationship with. A decent man who her brother wouldn't want to chop into pieces for messing with his sister."

"Listen to you. So worried about her long-term relationship success and happiness. And what about us isn't decent?"

"Maybe we could ask for something else in return," Dalton says, looking up thoughtfully, completely avoiding my question.

"Oh yeah? And what would that be?" I roll my shoulders as a grin lights up my brother's face like New Year's fireworks.

"Maybe she could cook us dinner. She cooks like her momma, you know. Travis told me."

It's at this point that I know my brothers have lost all their fucking sense. "You're seriously suggesting that a girl like Gabby will not only want to take us up on our offer of a three-sausage buffet, but also want to make us dinner in return. What kind of world are you living in because it isn't the real one?"

Blake turns to the closet, pulling open the door before he swivels back to me and grins. "I'm living in the world where I know what's in Gabby's diary. She wants us. All of us."

I glance at the door to the bathroom, my mouth dropping open at Blake's admission, wondering what Gabby's doing in her room right now. My cock stirs at how close that sweet pussy is. How close she is. I adjust my cock who's come so close to paradise but has to remain confined to my snug boxer briefs. "You read her diary?" I ask with disgust.

"Not me. Travis. He thought it was hilarious that she had a teenage crush on the three of us."

"That's because he never imagined we'd do anything about it."

"She's not a kid anymore," Dalton says. "And Blake's right. If she's that thirsty, and it's not us, it could be someone a whole lot worse."

"That's it, bro. Sell yourself," Blake laughs, tossing Travis's Yoda pillow at Dalton's head.

"We care about her, right?" Dalton rubs his beard, as a flush paints the skin over the top of his cheeks. "We'd do good by her."

"Hell yeah," Blake agrees, pulling out a pile of the sketchiest looking dirty magazines I've ever seen and dropping them on the bed. "Travis doesn't need to know because there won't be feelings involved. At least, not from her side. The diary said nothing about our winning personalities. She's just hooked up on our ripped bodies and rugged good looks. This might be our only chance to know what it'd be like to have a girl like Gabby."

I stare at my brothers, blinking slowly as their crazy, harebrained idea settles around us. If it's not us, it could be someone else who doesn't care for and respect her like we do. It could be so much worse.

The one-eighty my mind has done over the past few minutes unnerves me, but what can I say? I've had a crush on Gabby since before I even knew what it was. And if we can be what she needs, even for a few months, that would be more than I've ever hoped for.

"Who's going to ask her?"

Blake and Dalton nod their heads, grinning like I just offered them a case of beer and a monster-sized sirloin. "You," they both say simultaneously.

Now I'm sure they've lost their minds.

2

GABRIELLA

"They did what?" Ellie gasps, her hands flying to her mouth and her eyes bugging out.

"Do I need to say it again?"

"They came into your room while you were…" Ellie wiggles her eyebrows and I cringe all over again.

"While my vibe was doing what vibes do best," I say, groaning as the image of Kain, Blake, and Dalton barreling into my room floods my mind in all its terrible glory.

"Why were they there? I don't get it."

"Apparently my asshole brother wanted them to clear his room to help Mom before she redecorates. He's never been thoughtful before, so my guess is he had something sketchy in there that he wanted to hide."

"Probably a monster porn collection, although who has physical porn anymore when you can access it all online?"

I sip my black coffee and lick my lips. "My brother has always been a collector. He started with comics and probably downgraded to smutty mags."

"It's always the quiet ones." Ellie smiles and glances over her shoulder at a rowdy table of football players. I know she's probably missing her own rowdy team. It was weird when she wasn't around last year and I'm bummed that we won't graduate at the same time, but it's awesome she's managed to come back and finish her studies, despite having a baby and a whole new life with her three sexy stepbrothers.

"Yeah, well, my three nosy neighbors left with their mouths hanging open."

"I bet they did. It's not every day you stumble across your friend's sister with her legs open."

I cringe again and then shake my head, frustrated. Yeah, it wasn't ideal to be caught out like that, but I'm a woman with needs that I'm perfectly able to take care of. I shouldn't be embarrassed about it. I'm sure their right hands are busy most nights if they're not dating. The thought of those three fine men handling their junk sends heat pooling in places I'd rather weren't warm right now.

"I guess it's Kain you're most bothered about." Ellie says. "You know, because you might bump into him. The other two work, don't they?"

"Yeah. Blake works over at Ink Factor 2 and Dalton's their father's right-hand man at their construction business."

"Construction and tattoos. Those are some seriously sexy jobs."

Ellie isn't wrong. Dalton's always been a big boy, but over the last year, he's filled out to ridiculous proportions. He'd give the Hulk a run for his money! I'm not a petite woman and I reckon he could lift me above his head with one arm. And Blake has always been wickedly sexy with his mischievous half-smile and steely gray eyes, but now he's half-covered in ink, he's practically sinful.

"What are you going to do when you see him?" Ellie asks.

I shrug because I haven't really considered it. "Glare

angrily, I guess."

Ellie's lips twitch. "You know, Colby used to tutor Kain. He always talks about him like he's a stand-up guy, and that means a lot coming from Colb."

"Stand-up guy, huh? He probably had one main body part that was standing to attention after yesterday."

"You know they all went home and jerked off over you!" Ellie chuckles and pulls off a section of chocolate muffin, popping it into her mouth with a flourish.

"That's the only orgasm they are getting from me," I snort.

Ellie leans forward, studying me with narrowed eyes. "Kain's a very good-looking man and if his brothers are anything like him, that's a trio of hotness right there."

"Your point?"

"My point is that once upon a time, you dared me to do something, and it changed my life. I'm wondering if fate is turning the tables on us here. I'm wondering if I should be daring you into action, too?"

I swallow the last of my bitter coffee and shake my head. "You know I don't need dares, sweetie."

"So, why have you never hooked up with any of them?" she asks. "Because if I ever had a hot neighbor, I know I'd been tempted…you know, before the triplets."

"Oh, I've been tempted." I don't elaborate because the details of how much I've lusted over the Nowak brothers would probably blow her mind.

Ever since I was a little girl, and they were scrawny boys with dirty knees and torn T-shirts, I've had a crush on them. I even used to write about it in my diary. But Travis drew a line in the sand many years ago and reiterated it when I went through puberty. No messing around with his friends.

Maybe he could sense something between us all. Maybe

he was worried about his friendship. Most likely, he thought it was his role to step into Dad's empty shoes to protect me. It doesn't seem to have sunk into his skull that I can stand on my own two feet perfectly well.

Ellie frowns, confusion twisting her lips. "You've been tempted and not done anything about it? That doesn't sound like you."

She's right. It doesn't. I would have gone to at least first base with anyone else by now.

"My brother has made them a no-go zone."

"And you listen to your brother? That would be a first."

She's right. We love each other, but we both have stubborn as our middle names and that leads to a whole lot of disagreement.

"I guess it's ingrained that they're off-limits."

"You're all adults," Ellie muses, then grins. "And I was going to ask which of the three is your favorite, but as I know from experience, it isn't always necessary to choose!"

"Yeah, you're just greedy." I snaffle the last bit of Ellie's muffin to make a point, although I'm not sure what that point is.

"Greed is good. My whole life proves that point."

She's right. It does. She has three awesome men who worship the ground she walks on, a baby boy who's cute as a button, and a home she's turning into a perfect family dwelling. It makes me want to be greedy too, but the Nowak brothers are too close to home. I mean, they're so close we used to toss paper airplanes with messages inside through each other's windows.

So close that I've caught Kain changing in front of his window a few too many times.

Those were good days.

My poor vibe had a lot less work to get me off on

those days.

That chiseled jaw, broad chest, rounded biceps and abs like a Greek hero hewn from marble. I've never cursed a window ledge more than when it blocked my view of all the good stuff below the waist. Damn, Kain is fine.

And then there's Dalton. He's bigger than his brother in a burly, lumberjack kind of way. Thicker muscle to Kain's leaner build. His brows are darker too, and his beard is thicker. His hands are so big, I swear he could tear trees from the ground and not break a sweat.

And Blake? He has an edginess to him. He's all smiles, but there's a darkness behind his eyes that tips him into devilish territory. Tattoos have always done it for me, and since Blake started work, he's slowly covering more of his gorgeous, ripped body with ink.

"You're thinking about them, aren't you?" Ellie says, grinning and shaking her head.

"I might be," I admit, pressing my lips together to stifle my smile.

"You know, there's a saying that I've always really liked," Ellie says.

"Oh yeah, and what is that?"

"While the cat's away, the mouse will play, except in your case, Travis is the cat and you are the mouse. You have nothing to lose."

She's right, of course. I don't really have anything to lose. Since we all traipsed through the awkward years of puberty, I haven't hung out with the Nowak brothers much. They've always been there, as Travis's buddies, though.

Now Travis is adulting in Germany, maybe it would be possible to find out if my brother's best friends are everything I've fantasized they are. Travis never has to find out. When he returns home, things can go back to the way they were.

We could go back to being neighbors who nod at each other as we cross paths. And whatever we do could just be relegated to memories we recall in the future when we're old and gray and feel better for reminiscing on the stupid things we did in our youth.

3

KAIN

When somebody touches my shoulder while I'm in the line in the cafeteria, I expect it to be one of my teammates, ready to ask me to grab them lunch too. When I whirl around to find Gabriella behind me, I'm momentarily lost for words.

She looks like a vision, with the sunlight streaming through the windows behind her and her golden hair hanging straight over her shoulders. She also looks way more amused than I'd have expected with our last encounter still fresh in both our minds.

"Is standing around with your mouth hanging open a new thing for you?" she asks, then uses her index finger to gently push my chin up until my lips are closed. "Better." She blinks her black-rimmed, almond-shaped eyes and folds in her lips to hide her smile.

My brain has seized up, realizing she's casually referencing yesterday's incident without anger or malice. In fact, Gabriella Cross seems positively amused.

Interesting.

"Well, to be fair to me, I had a good reason yesterday."

"Yeah, you did." Her cheeks pink, making her appear a little more human. Even so, I'm still a little in awe of her from this close. All the years of thinking she's pretty are coiled up in my belly, ready to unsettle me.

"So, I should probably apologize profusely and explain why we burst into your room unannounced like three Neanderthals."

"It's okay," she says, raising her hands. "Mom told me that you were helpfully clearing Travis's room, and I wasn't the quietest. I guess you were coming to my aid."

I snort, taking two paces to the left to catch up with the others in the line. "Not the kind of aid you needed, though." The words come out before my brain has computed how they sound, and now it's my turn to blush. Well, I'm not sure it's even possible for me to blush. Too much beard and the tan I carry year-round from all the outdoor training I do.

"Yeah," she says, and if I'm not mistaken, her voice has taken a breathy turn.

Blake's suggestion barrels through my mind as I'm asked what I want by the server. "Burger and fries," I say. "And whatever she's having."

"Same," Gabriella says, and we both watch as our lunch is heaped messily together.

My stomach rumbles noisily at the sight of cooked food. It's not going to be that delicious. I know from experience. The bun is powdery and the patty too smooth. The fries have been sitting under warming lights so have lost their crisp. But it's better than anything we make at home.

I recall Dalton's ridiculous suggestion that we ask Gabby to cook for us with embarrassment. I'm embarrassed that I would love it to happen. How pathetic is that?

Taking both plates, I rest them together on my tray. It's

presumptuous to assume she'll sit with me because I pay for her lunch, but I'm hopeful. It suddenly seems ridiculous that I've known this girl since she wore onesies that sagged with her diapers, and we go to the same university and never hang out.

Maybe that's about to change.

"So, Blake and Dalton send apologies too," I say, wanting to turn the conversation back to yesterday.

"That's sweet," she says. "I don't need apologies, though. Just don't tell my brother."

Shooting her a serious look, I shake my head. "We would never mention it to anyone."

"Okay. Good."

I pay for the food and head to an empty table by the windows, and Gabriella trails behind me. When I take a seat, she does too, and I say an internal prayer of thanks to whichever deity has shined a lucky light on me today.

When I pass Gabriella her plate, she reaches out for it with two hands. "I'm going to demolish this," she says. "I'm ravenous."

There's a roughness to her voice that has my dick stirring between my legs. He'd like her to be ravenous too, just not about that kind of meat.

Travis, forgive me. What kind of friend am I, sitting in front of my best friend's sister, imagining her feasting on my sausage with as much gusto as she's using to handle her burger?

A terrible friend.

A terrible friend who's listened to his brother's crazy ideas and wants them to be reality more than he wants to win the next game.

"Be careful where your dick leads you," my dad told me when I turned thirteen. "*Your dick can be your best friend or your worst enemy. Just make sure he isn't the one making your*

decisions, or he'll get you into trouble." I laughed at him, thinking his tirade of advice sounded ridiculous. I was too young to grasp the concept of powerful desire. I was too foolish to grasp the power that comes with wanting a woman so much you'd sacrifice sense and loyalty and self-respect. But now, sitting with a burger clutched in my hands and the object of almost all of my fantasies sitting in front of me, I understand the wisdom of my old man.

Maybe my dick can be my best friend and my worst enemy at the same time if I let him get his way, and Gabriella doesn't have a shit-fit at the suggestion.

That's probably what will happen if I dare to voice what me and Blake and Dalton have wanted for more years than I can count. Not probably. Definitely. I mean, what kind of suggestion is it? Hey Gab, want to play pass the sausage with me and my douchebag brothers?

Even suggesting it would probably be construed as an insult.

It's not that we're not appealing prospects. I'm not oblivious to the longing looks we all get when we're out. There are enough jersey chasers on this campus to keep my bed filled every night. The thing is, none of them measure up to Gabriella. Not even close.

"So, are you dating?" she asks, breaking my downwardly spiraling train of thought.

"No." The single word sounds more abrupt than I meant it to, and her eyebrows pull up in surprise.

"And your brothers?"

"Dalton is too busy hefting bricks, and Blake works ridiculous hours. With my training schedule, we spend most of our downtime on our couch, exhausted."

"All work and no play." Gabriella pops a fry into her mouth and chews with a half-smile.

"Yeah, we have some time to play. We just haven't been lucky enough to find someone worth playing with."

Across the canteen, Elias and Dornan are having some kind of disagreement. I'd usually step in to intervene, but I'm not risking losing my spot with Gab. Let someone else break up their stupid rivalry.

"Someone?" she says. "Like, you're looking for just one woman between the three of you?"

I lower the burger, realizing my slip, and then take on board what the beautiful girl in front of me asked without a hint of disgust in her voice.

"Your best friend shares three dudes, right?" I ask, knowing full well that Ellie is in a committed relationship with Colby, Seb, and Micky. It's deflection but relevant.

"Yeah. I like to think I played a major hand in that blissful union."

That surprises me. "Really. What did you do?"

"It all started with a dare," she says, glancing over her shoulder as though she's worried someone might be listening to our conversation. "I mean, I knew Ellie had a thing for her stepbrothers for a while, so I nudged her in the right direction."

"Maybe your momma should have named you Cupid."

Gabriella winks and wiggles her eyebrows and I drop my head from side to side, suddenly feeling the need to limber up. It's like the minutes before a big game when a surge of nervous anticipation makes my skin tingle and my head hot.

"To be honest, I thought she would get down and dirty with one of them and that would be it. I never imagined she'd sleep with them all."

"Well, sometimes sex is just sex," I say. "And sometimes it comes with feelings."

"Awe, listen to you, Mr. Big Bad Baller, getting all emotional."

I pick up a fry and toss it at her. "It isn't the nineteen-fifties, you know. Men don't have to be made of stone anymore."

"I always took you for a tough guy," she says. "Remember when Tommy pulled my pigtails in our front yard? You punched him so hard you made his nose bleed."

"I was nine," I snort. "But I'd do it again now if anyone messed with you."

Gabriella rests her hand over her chest, drawing my attention to the soft skin of her neck and clavicle, and the curve of her breast beneath her black tank. "Be still my heart."

"I kind of like the idea that I made it race."

I lean forward a little and Gabriella holds my gaze, almost as though she's staring into my soul and trying to work out if I'm worthy. I'm grateful she doesn't really have that kind of X-ray vision because who knows what she'd discover? I try to be a good, respectable man, but the thoughts I've had about this girl would send me straight into Satan's furnace.

She folds in her pretty lips, the full bottom one looking glossy and appealing as it's released. Damn, if we were alone, and she was willing, I could kiss the hell out of her. And more. So much more.

She leans in too, the space between us feeling charged with a new kind of energy. "I was telling Ellie what happened," she whispers. "She asked me if I ever thought about you guys in *that* way." She inclines closer when she emphasizes *that* and I lean in too, sensing this could be a pivotal moment between us. The kind of moment I don't want to waste or forget.

Maybe Blake wasn't so crazy with his suggestion. Maybe Gabriella really wants us.

"And what did you say?"

"I told her that despite Travis defining you all as off-limits, it didn't stop me from wondering."

I feel bad for knowing just how much wondering she's done over the years. Travis divulged a whole lot of Gab's journal to Blake, and I don't like the unequal footing it puts us on. "Wondering?" God, I'm making her work for this, but I have to. The closer we get to admitting the forbidden, the more I need to know for sure it's what she wants. If the shit ever hits the fan in the future, it could make all the difference.

"Yeah," she whispers, her pupils spreading wide and aroused, and it takes every ounce of restraint I possess to not climb over the stupid fucking table and grab this woman. "Wondering what it might be like. Haven't you wondered?"

"I'm a man, Gab," I say. "Wondering is part of our DNA. There's isn't much time in the day when we're not wondering." She laughs, and the sound makes my heart expand against my ribs. "When you wondered, what was it like?" My voice comes out as husky as it gets after I've yelled my lungs out at a game, and I flex my fingers beneath the table, my half-eaten burger and fries forgotten as the woman of my dreams confesses that I've not been alone in what I thought were off-limits fantasies.

"Good," she says, biting her bottom lip. "So good."

"Fuck…" Below the table, my cock stirs, eager and ready and my heart speeds, thudding in the cavity of my chest like a drum warning of invaders.

"You ever think about doing more than just wondering?" Her eyes search for an answer I might not confess, but I'm beyond all thoughts of why this is so fucking wrong. Gabriella Cross may be my best friend's little sister, but she's all woman and so far, my greatest fucking temptation.

"Shit, Gab. What are you trying to do to me?" I groan.

"Tease you to the point of distraction," she grins, biting her lip again.

"Only tease? I thought you were an angel, not a devil."

"Oh, I'm a devil when it counts."

She leans back, resting against the chair, the extra distance between us feeling all wrong. I need her closer. So close, we're skin on skin, heat on heat, sweat on sweat. One being fixated on nothing but pleasure. But she's making it very obvious that flirting is as far as she's going to take this.

If I want her, I'm going to have to work for her. But that's not a problem. I'd toil until the end of time just for a chance to see again what I saw by accident yesterday.

"I think we should hook up," I say before I can convince myself to keep my distance. "In fact, I'm sure we should hook up. No way that bit of rubber is doing what a woman like you needs. Frankly, it's a travesty that you should ever need to resort to battery powered satisfaction."

"Kain Nowak, are you propositioning me?" She feigns shock, her hand pressing against her mouth even as her eyes dance with excitement.

"Look at it as me offering you a service. Whenever you need me, just drop me a message and I'll be there to rock your world."

"Dial-a-dick!" she laughs.

"I guess you could call it that."

"What would your brothers think?" she asks.

"Well, that's the thing," I say, already cringing at what I'm going to need to bring to the conversation. "It's all of us or none of us." Holding my breath, I watch Gabriella chew the inside of her cheek. She's going to say no. She's going to tell me I'm a degenerate fucker. She's going to tell Travis and blow up our friendship into the stratosphere, nuclear style.

"Triple dial-a-dick," she laughs eventually, and I know for certain that I've never been more relieved to hear the sweet tinkle of her amusement in my life.

"Three for the price of one," I agree.

"A bargain," she laughs, picking up her burger. "I better start fueling up."

As she eats, I realize we've talked about this, but she hasn't actually agreed. She's left me out on a limb, hanging in the wind. I'm not going to push it, though. Women don't like men who beg. They want a man so confident he'll assume he's desirable enough that she'll definitely say yes.

"You'd better keep your strength up because there's another part to this offer."

"Oh yeah? What?"

"Well, in repayment for our dial-a-dick services, you'll need to cook for us. A home cooked meal for every orgasm."

She splutters, choking on whatever was in her mouth. I pass her a bottle of water so she can wash down her food and a napkin to dry her lips. "I can't agree to that," she says.

"Why not?"

"Because I'm banking on you guys working hard, and that's going to mean more big O's than there are mealtimes."

Shit. She's banking…it hits me that she's agreed to the part of this arrangement that matters.

Fuck Dalton's stupid food idea. We can live on sandwiches for the rest of our lives.

Or maybe not.

"Okay. Let's say four hot meals a week in exchange for an unlimited number of orgasms."

Our eyes meet and the zap of heat that passes between us sends shivers over my spine and a surge of blood into my cock.

"Four meals I can do, but you'll have to buy the ingredients."

"Done," I say, offering my hand.

She takes it, wrapping her cool, slender fingers around mine and shaking vigorously. "Nice doing business with you, Mr. Nowak." She grins.

"Nice doing business with you, Miss Cross."

And just like that, it seems that all my fantasies might come true after all.

4

GABRIELLA

It's 9 pm when my phone buzzes. When I swipe open my phone, I discover I've been invited to a new WhatsApp group called Dial-A-D. Very cute.

I guess Kain has had a chance to communicate the details of our discussion to his big brothers and that they are in agreement. I turn to face the long-arched mirror that's propped in the corner of my bedroom, gazing at the girl who thought it would be a good idea to step into forbidden territory.

Forbidden because they're my brother's best friends in the world and forbidden because there are three of them.

My reflection stares back, stripped of makeup, dressed in one of Travis's worn shirts that is so oversized on me that it hangs past my thighs.

I've always tried to be a brave girl. I guess being surrounded by boys from a young age drove me to be more daring, trying to keep up with their constant drive for crazy adventures. Since I started University, I've had my fair share of flings with varying degrees of satisfaction. Most of the time, after a couple of dates, I back out. As soon as I smell a whiff of too much interest from them,

I'm out the door.

I like my men cool and in charge, preferably okay with holding me at arm's length with a slightly frosty exterior and a domineering side that keeps me grounded.

My go-to romance novels always involve a dominant book boyfriend of some sort; a CEO who seduces his assistant, a mafia don who kidnaps his rival's sister, a motorcycle club criminal who rescues a woman from violence and then proceeds to keep her captive for himself. They're all equally cold at the start, sometimes with a nasty streak and enjoy a little pain.

So far, none of my fellow students have come close to being the kind of man who could really get me off and hold me down for more than a passing interlude.

Blake - Gabs! I heard you're up for replacing your rabbit with my snake. Hit me up whenever.

Dalton - Seriously, dude! That's what you go with as an introduction to this? Gabs, I just clipped him around the back of the head on your behalf.

Blake - He did, with his big orc hand.

Kain - Guys, can you tone down the bullshit? For fuck's sake.

Kain - Gabs, as you can see, I've filled in my idiot brothers on the arrangement. I'm sure you can tell from Blake's eloquent message, they're in. I guess all there is to say is that we're at your beck and call. Whenever you need us, use this chat. Whoever is around will fulfill whatever desire you have. When you don't need us anymore, all you have to do is leave this chat and we'll know. No expectations. No hard feelings. Just fun between friends, okay?

I reply with a simple OK, and three smiley-face emojis appear in quick succession.

Gab - anyone free before classes tomorrow? My mom leaves home at 8 am. My classes start at 11 am.

Kain - Me. I'll come to you.

Dalton - He's going to bring some ingredients too.

Kain - Dalton went shopping already. He's more excited about the food than the sex.

Dalton - I'm not, Gab.

Dalton - Kain, you're a douche!

Dalton - But a man's gotta eat, especially when he's grafting all day.

Blake - Here we go again! Are you ever going to shut up about the bricks?

Kain - Guys, we should leave Gabriella now. See you tomorrow.

More smiley emojis light up my screen and I can't stop smiling at their goofy back-and-forth. It's been a long time since I've been included in their friendship with Travis, and I miss the fun we used to have.

But now it's something else too. Between my legs, my pussy has a level of sexual awareness that it hasn't had in weeks. My clit tingles, aching to be touched, and lower, I'm heavy and achy. It would be so easy to pull out my vibe, but I'm going to wait. I want to really feel the need for what Kain is going to give me tomorrow. I want him and his brothers to own my pleasure while this agreement is in place, because isn't that the point of it?

It's still early, so I take a seat at my desk to finish an assignment that's due by the end of the week, but I'm easily distracted by the memory of Kain's body, seen furtively through a crack in my drapes. What will it be like to touch him? To feel the heat of his skin, and the beat of his heart. To know what he tastes like. To know how he likes to fuck.

Instead of focusing, I come up with all kinds of imaginary Kains, whispering imaginary filthy things in my ear, holding me down, forcing my mouth deep onto his cock. I drive myself crazy until my panties are damp and my body is tingly.

When my phone beeps again, it's like I've been woken from a deep sleep.

Kain - Are you thinking about it?

Fuck. His message is private, away from the group chat.

Me - Yeah. How could I not? This is big.

Kain - It is big. *wink emoji* Tell me what you like. I want to make your fantasies come true.

Fuck. Fuck.

Is he serious? No man has ever asked me that before. No man has ever cared to find out what's inside my mind before they've tried to get inside my body. This is sexy. Like, really sexy. Any reservations that I've been clinging to melt away. I owe it to myself to be honest.

Me - Take charge. Tell me what to do. Manhandle me. Show me your strength.

I can see he's typing for a while, and I wait, nibbling a hangnail, desperate for the message to deliver. What if he thinks I'm fucked up? What if he's secretly submissive? Just because he's a brute on the football field and built like a brick wall doesn't mean he's an animal in the bedroom.

When my phone beeps, I close my eyes and say a silent prayer.

My prayer is answered.

Kain - That's what I like, too.

Wow. Just wow.

Kain - Just promise me you'll tell me if I cross any lines, okay?

I place my hand over my heart, pleased at his sensitivity, the butterflies in my belly resting a little with a new feeling of confidence.

It's not that I doubted that Kain, Blake, or Dalton

would treat me well. They're good men raised by a strong father. He might not have taught them basic domestic skills, but he educated them on respect. They're big and rough, but gentlemen at heart.

It's more that I didn't expect the communication.

Me - I will. Thanks for saying it.

Kain - Of course. Don't forget, this is about you. We're at your service.

I send a blushing emoji, my own cheeks hot. How am I going to get through tonight feeling this needy? I guess it's going to take some serious willpower.

When my alarm goes off at 7 am, I leap from my bed in a way that's completely out of character for me. Forget snoozing this morning, I need to get ready for Kain's imminent arrival and that means showering, and all the other beauty treatments necessary for a first time with someone. Rather than feeling exhausted in the shower like I usually do, I bounce on my feet and sing a very out of tune version of my favorite song, shampooing my hair and rubbing my skin with expensive, special occasion exfoliator until it's softer than a baby's butt.

By the time I emerge from my steam bubble, I'm pink cheeked and buzzing. Choosing what to wear seems like a waste of time, seeing as I'm going to be peeled out of it soon, but I'm not going to open the door naked.

For a second, I imagine Kain's expression if I did just that, but even with all my confidence, I'm not quite ready to be that brazen. Maybe next time.

I decide to go with a white lacy bra and panties with little ribbons securing them at the hips. When I've put a wave into my hair, I look positively innocent, which seems fitting considering our little text chat.

Maybe he'll like pretending it's my first time and he's

the one plundering my innocence. In a way, I wish he was. My real first time was a major disappointment. A lot of huffing and puffing on Ben's part and zero enjoyment on mine.

When I spray my favorite perfume on my pulse points, I shiver with anticipation.

At 8 am, Mom yells her goodbyes up the stairs, and I tug on a cute blue pajama set which will be easy to remove.

I check my phone a million times, half expecting to receive a message from Kain telling me he's not coming, swayed by a last-minute prick of conscience about having his wicked way with his best friend's baby sister.

Except I'm not a baby anymore.

By the time I've made a quick protein smoothie for breakfast and consumed it in record time, the doorbell rings.

Oh god.

He's here. No conscience stopping him, or at least, if there is, it's not enough to keep him away.

When I finally open the door, there's no going back. I know, as soon I see his sapphire eyes, framed by thick dark lashes that no man should have any business possessing, I'll be lost.

I pad to the door, my bare feet almost noiseless. When my hand touches the handle, I have to inhale deeply to steady my rising nerves.

Pulling the door open slowly, I brace myself for the impact of Kain, but it's futile. He looks like a god; dark hair still damp from the shower, a white tee that tugs across his impossibly broad, muscular chest like its threads are fighting a war to remain untorn. Thick thighs strain at his snug blue joggers. My eyes drift over him hungrily and without any embarrassment, it seems. I lick my lips and when I finally meet his gaze, Kain is smiling, with dancing eyes.

He's amused. "Gabriella." A simple nod of greeting, and the reverberation of his deep voice jolts me out of my daze.

"Kain." I usher him to come in, sweeping the street outside quickly to check for nosy neighbors. We're good.

The click of the door closing is shockingly loud, and then the silence of the house envelops us. Kain looks around a hallway that should be familiar, but the way he focuses on the photographs, it's like he's seeing everything for the first time.

"I miss those days." He raises his head in the direction of an image of us when we were kids, standing together in the backyard. All the boys, Travis, Kain, Dalton, and Blake, have their arms around each other. I'm standing slightly to the left of Kain, dressed in a short green dress, with my hair pulled into long braids.

"Life was simpler," I agree.

"Yeah." He folds in his bottom lip, pinching it between his teeth, then, as if he forgot he was carrying a bag of groceries, he nods toward them. "Shall I put these in the kitchen?"

"Sure." it feels very weird to follow this hunk of a man, who's here to fuck me senseless, into the kitchen to talk dinner. "What did you bring?"

"Chicken thighs and a bunch of vegetables."

"Perfect." I switch the oven on and grab a tray.

"You're going to do this now?" He seems surprised.

"If you want cooked food by the time you leave, we need to get it into the oven right now."

"Okay."

I take the bag from his hands and unload everything onto the counter. I grab my mom's huge box of seasonings and herbs, and some oil. It doesn't take long for me to chop the onions, bell peppers, zucchini, and potatoes into chunks. While I'm busy, Kain leans against the counter, watching with fascination. I toss them all into a big square stainless-steel pan, add enough oil to coat, and a mix of seasoning that I know is going to make everything taste delicious with a hint of heat. The chicken is added on top and then I toss it all around with my hands so that everything is mixed. "This is a one-pan meal," I say. "The effort is in the preparation, and then you just leave it to cook."

"So we don't have to watch it?"

"Nope," I say, covering the whole thing in foil and setting it into the warmed oven. I'll set a timer on my phone, and we'll cook it slowly to give us enough time. My heart skips a beat in my chest as Kain takes a step closer.

"Enough time, huh?"

His thumb brushes across my lips, creating a shiver of nerves that run up the back of my neck and over my scalp. He's so close that the scent of his skin makes me woozy. Oh God, what have I gotten myself into with this man and his brothers?

A whole pot of delicious danger.

"Yeah." I tip my chin up defiantly and Kain chuckles.

"Better get up those stairs." It's a mild order, but I feel it between my legs like he just spread them and licked a long hot stripe.

"Yes, sir," I whisper, loving the way his eyes lower at my submission.

Kain follows me up the stairs that we've scrambled up as kids, his presence looming with intent behind me. At the top, we both pause, the sight of Travis's door making this feel even more forbidden.

My brother would hate this.

He'd be furious with us both.

He'd be disgusted that his best friends have hatched

this plan. Disgusted that they waited until he was out of the country to do the very thing he forbade.

But Travis isn't here, and even though I love my brother more than life itself, I know he doesn't have any right to control who I fuck. In case Kain is feeling the frost of cold feet, I reach back and take his hand in mine, leading him to my childhood bedroom.

The walls were once pink and lined with dolls and stuffed animals. I updated it to something more fitting for a college-aged woman two years ago and I'm thankful I did. It's now nothing like it used to be when I'd force Kain to play Barbie and Ken with me.

I distract myself by setting up the timer while Kain closes the door and slides the lock in place. Even though we're alone in the house, it makes sense to prepare for the worst.

When we turn to face each other, my mouth goes as dry as ash.

"Take off your top."

I open my mouth to say something, but nothing comes out. My arms, controlled by the strict tone of Kain's instructions, lift the hem until it's over my head and I'm left in my lacy bra and pajama shorts.

Kain inhales a deep breath that broadens his chest even further. "And the shorts."

I take my time to slide them over my hips, holding his gaze, watching as his eyes darken to the color of the sky before a storm. Kain widens his stance, and his big, right hand slowly moves to cup his cock.

As soon as the fabric pools at my feet, he orders me to turn and the rumble he makes when he sees my ass is primal. "Come here, Gabriella."

It's in my nature to be defiant. To tell him no. If you want me, you come here. But having Kain Nowak at my beck and call wouldn't be half as much fun as submitting to his will. Drawing my shoulders back, I take four steps, leaving a foot between us. In a flash, he closes that gap, his hand securing the back of my neck and his mouth punishing mine in a bruising kiss. The passion, the frenzy; it's like a pot of longing that's been filling for years has suddenly been tipped.

My hands claw at his shoulders, his arms, his back, wanting closeness. He lifts me by the ass, wrapping my legs around his hips, supporting me as though I weigh nothing. The huge bar of his cock lies along the seam of my pussy, driving me crazy. When he turns, pinning my body between him and the cool plaster, I gasp. His hips press onto mine and I whimper as my clit swells.

Freeing a hand, he palms my breast, finding it soft enough to make him groan, teasing the nipple until it's a ravaged point.

"You don't know how long I've wanted this," he mouths against my neck. "How long I've imagined the taste of you on my tongue."

"Me too," I gasp.

His hand grasps my jaw, holding my face tightly and staring intently. "You want to taste me?"

"Yes," I whisper.

Kain lowers me so my feet hit the cool floor, then his hand is on my shoulder, urging me to my knees. He shoves at the waist of his joggers and pulls out his cock, gripping it with a ferocity that looks painful, moaning as he uses the tip to trace my lips. "Open up, Gabriella. Show me that sweet tongue."

I loosen my jaw, staring up into his ever-darkening eyes as he slides his perfect cock into my mouth, his fingers still gripping the root. He didn't lie. It really is big.

His thighs tremble with restraint as I wrap my lips around his girth and hollow my cheeks, the salt-sweetness of his pre-come making me light-headed.

"Good girl," he whispers, easing forward, pressing into the back of my throat with just enough control that I don't gag. As his hips ease back, I rest my hand against the rounded perfection of his football-trained honed butt and moan around his cock. "Fuck," he curses, as I take him deeper. "Fuck."

His hand cups the back of my head, not to force but to give the impression of control which dampens my panties. By the time Kain fucks me, I'm going to be a slippery mess.

With each thrust, I open my throat, taking Kain so deep my nose brushes the neatly trimmed hair encircling his cock, and his eyes become almost frantic. I can make him come this way, with just a little swallow reflex and a well-timed vibrating moan, but maybe he won't want that. Maybe he'll want to save his release until he's inside me. Or maybe he'll like me to watch him spray it all over my stomach. Any of those options sound amazing to me.

"I'm going to come," he says so deeply that my toes curl. "Do you want to swallow?"

I nod, already feeling the taste of his cock intensify with each pass. He doesn't get rougher with his thrusts. In fact, the perfect control he exerts over himself is something to witness. Instead, his grip in my hair intensifies until it's almost too painful, and then he releases, hot and slick into my throat, his face tipped to the heavens like he's thanking the almighty for the epic release. His cock slides from my lips and I swallow like the good girl I want to be for him. I rest my hands on my knees, taking an obedient position in the shadow of his powerful frame as his fingers tease my hair and he tucks himself away.

"You look good on your knees for me," he murmurs, through a throat that sounds constricted with pleasure. "But it's time to get up." He holds out his hands and I slide mine into his grip, allowing him to help me to my feet, feeling tiny even when I'm standing up to my full height. Kain's finger lazily traces my clavicle and then lower, to the lace cups of my bra.

"You look so sweet and innocent dressed like this," he murmurs.

"Is that what you like?"

He kisses me again then, his tongue slick against mine, showing me just how much he likes it. With a firm grip, he takes both my wrists, forcing my hands behind my back and securing them in one hand. With the other, he grasps my jaw, tipping my face to his.

My legs tremble with arousal and anticipation as Kain makes his ability to overpower me obvious. This is what I want. It's what I need. It's something I've never found with any other man.

How far will he take it?

I hope all the way.

"This body is mine," he whispers darkly. "Your perfect tits, mine. Your soft lips, mine. That deep throat, mine to use. And your pussy…" Kain pauses for effect, glancing down between us to where I'm squeezing my thighs together. "I'm going to ruin your pussy for any other man."

"What about your brothers?" I whisper, forcing my chin higher with defiance.

"They're going to ruin your pussy too," he growls.

With quick action, he pushes me two paces until the back of my legs touch the mattress. Keeping a grip on my face and hands, he lowers me until my back touches the soft white comforter and remains over me, staring as though he can't quite believe what we're doing. For effect, I struggle a little, trying to pull my hands free, but they remain perfectly in his expert hold. "We can do this the easy way or the hard way," he whispers, his words tickling the tips of my nipples. "You can keep your hands behind your back like a good girl, or I can tie them up?"

"I'll keep them there," I say quickly, wanting to please him. Needing him to know that I relent to his demands. There will be other days when I'll let him bind me.

His fingers disengage from my wrists, easing out from behind my body. He presses a harsh kiss to my mouth before he pushes up on his arms, biceps bulging, his shirt pulling taut. When he straightens, he pulls the tee over his head with one hand in a move that I wish I had captured on video for all eternity.

Shit. Kain should be illegal. He looks too good. Smells too good. *Feels* too good.

He tosses the shirt onto the floor, his eyes never leaving mine. "Put your feet on the bed."

My body snaps to attention, doing as he's ordered, even though it will leave my legs open and my pussy spread behind the flimsy fabric of my panties.

"That's it," he says. "Perfect."

One thick finger trails from my knee, down the inside of my thigh, and I struggle to stay still, fighting a losing battle against my body's responses.

"Still," he barks, and I jump, holding my back in its unnaturally arched position, anchoring my abdominals to remain as motionless as possible.

His finger continues its trail, bypassing my pussy and following the path to my navel. He touches the piercing I have there, a tiny diamond stud. "Blake will love this. Outside tattoos, piercings are his other great love." His voice is soft when he talks about his brother, which reminds me of their unwavering bond. Most siblings have arguments, but the Nowaks never did more than bicker. They don't look alike, but they're closer than peas in a pod.

Higher, he touches the front fastening of my bra. "It's time we lost this," he says.

"Yes," I whisper.

With an expert flick, my bra is undone, and the fabric is

eased from my skin.

The sigh Kain makes is like pure satisfaction. "You have the prettiest tits," he says. "Better than I imagined."

"You imagined?"

"Fuck yeah." He bends forward, mouth hovering just above my right nipple. His breath tickles my skin, drawing the already pointed tip tighter. His hot tongue flicks over, once, twice, and then his hungry mouth latches on and sucks, hard.

Fuck. I tip my head back, no longer able to maintain the eye contact Kain has kept, needing to drift into a place where my body takes over from my mind.

His big hand palms my other breast, rough and hard. Perfect.

The tug of his mouth sends a pulse of connection between my legs, and I force my thighs together, needing contact.

Quick as a flash, Kain taps my hip. "Keep your legs open."

I whimper, understanding he wants to frustrate me, loving it and hating it in equal measure. He's slow to travel down the length of my body, but with every kiss, every lick, every nuzzle, I quiver more with anticipation.

When his lips are pressed to the soft, rounded part of my lower belly, I push up on my heels, raising my hips to urge him forward. "What do you need, baby?" he murmurs. "What do you want?"

"Touch me," I gasp. "Make me come."

"Oh, that's exactly what I'm going to do."

With two tugs, the ribbons at the side of my panties are undone. Kain presses my knees apart, spreading my pussy wide, staring down at my most private place with eyes that burn with desire. He licks his index finger and runs it over my clit, and I almost burst with just that one tiny touch.

"Slowly," he teases, easing my hips back to the bed. "There's no rush. I'm going to give you what you want, and it'll be so much better for waiting."

"Please," I beg, seeing how much he likes it. "Don't make me wait."

"Baby, baby. This pussy's so hungry, isn't it?"

I nod; my mouth suddenly dries as his finger traces lower and lower, the thick tip resting against my entrance. "Please." I shift again, so quickly that I take his finger inside me just an inch and he groans at the same time as me. It's enough for him to lose some of the tightly coiled restraint he's been teasing me with.

When his rough tongue strokes against my clit, I buck against his mouth, but when he pushes that finger up against my G-spot, my toes curl. "That's it," he says, flicking his tongue faster, forcing his finger deeper and harder. "Come for me, Angel."

And I do. Oh I do. My thighs snap closed around his head, and I moan so deeply it vibrates my lips. I think I'm going to pass out from the racing of my heart, but then I hear the tear of a foil packet and the slick sounds of a condom rolling, and I know I need to come to my senses because Kain is getting ready for more.

5

KAIN

There's an angel spread out on the bed before me. A real fucking angel.

Gabriella Cross, the most perfect woman on the planet, just came against my tongue. I felt her pussy clamp down on my fingers, I tasted her arousal, I heard her cries.

Every dream I ever had about Gab just came true.

Well, maybe not every dream. There are things I've fantasized about doing with this girl that aren't part of this agreement. Lazy mornings in bed, afternoons watching movies and eating popcorn, and date nights and fancy restaurants. They can't be a part of our future.

I don't want to focus on that, though. I want to gaze down at the gorgeous woman in front of me, and relish making this a reality.

"You can take your hands out now," I say, assisting Gabs to free herself. She flexes her fingers and reaches up to take my hand.

It's a moment of sweetness. A connection that feels outside a cool arrangement focused on pleasure. A moment of affection I relish.

"I always thought you'd be big," she whispers, and her cheeks flush adorably.

"You thought about my cock?" My brows pinch together, surprised but mostly pleased that I've not been the only one perving in this relationship. I tap her hip, not wanting to disappoint her by failing to deliver on her fantasy. Keeping my voice low and cold, I issue an order. "Shuffle back."

Gabriella centers herself on her big white bed like a princess in a fairytale; Sleeping Beauty awakened and ravenous. She's in the same position she was when I burst into her room, but this time I get to touch her. I get to be the one to make her come.

Damn, I can't wait to slide between her soft thighs and feel that sweet pussy clamp down around my big cock. I can't wait to fill her and feel her body tremble, resist, and eventually give way.

I can't wait to own what I thought could never be mine, even if it's just for today. Who knows how long she'll want this agreement to last? Who knows how many more chances I'll get to experience paradise?

I climb over her, roughly nudging her knees apart until her legs are spread wide enough to accommodate my bulk. She's a tall girl, but beneath me, she seems tiny. Her blue eyes blink, the pupils like dark jewels in the center. Her hands tentatively touch my arms and shoulders, roaming lower until they rest just above my ass.

I could slap them away or grip her wrists in mine. I think she'd like that, and I'd like it, too, but there's something about her touching me that's better than control. I just hope she thinks so too.

"You ready, princess?"

She looks between us, at the place where my cock hangs menacingly, a huge bar that seems capable of violent intention.

"You really think that's going to fit inside me?" she asks.

Shit, that's a question every man wants to hear. I smirk, raising my eyebrows.

"You wanted dick. You're getting dick." I kiss her, devouring her pouty lips, tasting her sweet mouth until I feel her relax. I grind against her sex with the underside of my cock, giving her just enough pressure to build arousal. She's wet from her last orgasm, but I want her ready and needy. I want her to crave this, to need me desperately.

My cock pulses, more than ready for what's coming, already recovered from the epic blowjob Gabriella gave me. Like the moments before I play football, my thighs bunch, and my glutes contract in readiness. I'm coiled so tight; I feel like I could run the length of the field without breaking a sweat.

As I slide my tongue against hers, gripping her face for that bite of control that she loves so much, I let my cock drop to notch at her little entrance. Maybe she was right to worry. She feels impossibly tight. I press forward, letting the full weight of my body rest behind my cock. Gabriella's fingernails dig into the skin of my shoulders. "It's okay, Princess," I whisper, gazing into her glazed eyes. "I've got you. Just relax. Let my big cock in and I promise you, he'll make you feel good."

I push forward again, relishing the resistance, but desperate to break through and spread her wide with my dick. I want to look down at the place we're joined and see me buried to the root. She'll take all of me. I know she will. I'll feed her every goddamned inch.

I watch as her mouth opens in awe.

Fuck.

I take her bottom lip in mine and bite down gently as her pussy loses the battle and succumbs to the pressure. She's so slick that I slide deep, and she gasps, her eyes rolling, her neck arching. "Oh fuck, Kain," she groans.

"Better than that fucking rubber stick?"

She nods. "Yes. Oh…so much better."

I move, withdrawing almost totally before I thrust back in, hard. Her groans draw my balls tighter and urge my thrusts. It feels so good to be inside this girl I've wanted since the first moment I realized girls were cool. It's like my whole world has flipped on its axis and everything that was missing is suddenly here, laid out in front of me.

"Give it to me," she gasps, and I thrust harder, taking my thumb and slicking it before I push it between us and press against her clit. Oh god, she's swollen. What was just a tiny nub is now totally exposed and straining for sensation. I keep going, watching her face contort with longing, as her body writhes beneath mine, desperate for release.

It's so hard to keep control when all I want to do is unleash everything inside her. All the pent-up yearning. All the fantasies becoming reality drive me on. I take hold of her hands, grinding against her clit as I hold her captive. With all control mine, her eyes glaze.

"You're mine, Angel. Mine. Don't ever forget it."

The words sound like dirty talk, but they leak from a place deep down inside me that craves it to be true. But I can pretend it's the kind of thing a man says to push his girl over the edge. Gabriella wants dominance. She wants to feel possessed as much as I want to possess her.

This is only temporary. The words whisper in my head, and I shake them away.

Focus on the fucking.

Make this girl come so hard she'll never want to seek pleasure in another man's bed.

Selfish, my mind whispers.

You want to ruin her for other men when you can't be the man she needs.

"Fuck," I gasp, as Gabriella tenses, her pussy constricting in wave after wave, her legs snapping so tight against my waist I have to slow my thrusts. I push her sweat-damp hair back from her flushed face, and kiss her parted lips, tasting the franticness of her breath and feeling the vibration of the soul-deep moan she makes when she's done.

Perfection.

There will never be another woman who'll make me feel this good. There will never be another woman who'll know me as well as Gabriella Cross. She's been with me through every major event in my life. I'll never forget the way she slid her hand into mine the day of Mom's funeral and didn't let go.

Today, her hands trail my shoulders and my back, resting against my ass and tugging me deeper. "Your turn," she whispers. "Give me everything you've got."

And fuck if that isn't the sexiest thing anyone's ever said to me.

I keep my eyes open as I work my hips, pushing so deep and hard that I shunt Gabriella up the bed and she has to hold on for dear life. I watch her eyes roll and relish the way she bites her lip as I get closer. Between us, we're sweat-slicked and hotter than the sun, and I'm sure Gabriella's hips must be aching. I take her legs and rest them over one of my shoulders, groaning at the additional depth and the way she gasps as I fold her in two. "That's it, baby," I say. "I'm going to give you every fucking bit of me."

And I do. Oh, I fucking do.

I come like a volcano that's been dormant for millennia, and shout loud enough to disturb the neighbors. Luckily, no one is at my house next door, and Mr. Grady, who lives on the other side, is almost deaf.

I pulse and pulse, filling the rubber, half worried I'm going to overspill. For a second, I fantasize about what it might be like with nothing between us. Gabriella would make beautiful babies, and mix them with my DNA, well, I'd like to imagine they'd be perfect.

Ridiculous thoughts to be having after the most spectacular orgasm of all time, but that's the place my mind wants to go when I'm still rutting in Gabriella's sweet little pussy, not wanting to accept that this morning between us is nearly over.

Just as I start to pull out, imagining kissing down her body and tasting between her legs, the phone alarm goes.

"Noooo…" I groan, and she giggles, swatting my shoulder and wriggling out from underneath me.

She slides off the bed, still laughing, and then disappears into a crumpled heap. Even though I'm still paralyzed with pleasure, I jump up to find her collapsed on the floor, holding her stomach as she laughs and laughs.

"What the hell, Gabriella?"

"My legs don't work," she splutters. "You turned them to jelly."

I bend and scoop her into my arms, feeling my heart swell and my chest expand with pride. "You mean I fucked the life out of you," I snort.

"Life. Bones. Who the fuck knows?" she laughs, burying her head against me. I kiss her hair and move to sit on the edge of the mattress.

"Here. Take a minute."

"The food will dry out," she moans, but quietens when I kiss her gently on the forehead.

"A woman shouldn't be jumping up from sex to deal with food in the oven."

"Says the man who bought the food."

"I blame Dalton."

She touches my face and wriggles her toes, testing. "You won't blame Dalton later when you're eating it."

"Now that is true."

"Let me try again," she says. Like a baby deer, I set her on long slender wobbly legs, and this time she manages to stand. I can't resist planting a kiss on her ass, and she jumps, surprised. "Kain Nowak, are you trying to give me a heart attack?"

"I'm trying to appreciate your ass," I say. "Or should I say *my* ass?"

She turns, still naked as the day she was born, gorgeous tits now pointed in my direction. Fuck. How am I going to leave this girl and function for a whole day at college? How am I going to leave space and time for my brothers to fulfill their part of the arrangement? How am I going to carry on living my life knowing the girl I always believed was perfect for me is in fact, completely ideal?

"I like you possessive," she whispers, bending to kiss my lips, then she grabs a shirt from the chair by her desk, throws it over her head and disappears through her bedroom door, bounding down the stairs like a herd of buffalo.

I tug on my joggers and shirt and follow, inhaling the delicious smell of the food Gabriella prepared.

"What do you think?" she asks, looking so cute with her giant pink oven mitts and bare feet vulnerable on the tiled floor.

The food in the tray is still sizzling; vegetables and chicken cooked to perfection. "I think it looks amazing," I say. "I think Dalton, in particular, is going to become your friend for life."

"I thought he already was," Gabriella says, her bottom lip protruding a little.

"Well, of course he is," I backtrack. "But this is going to seal the deal."

She places the tray on a wooden board on the countertop and pulls some aluminum foil from an overhead cupboard, wrapping the food like she's tucking a child into bed.

"You can take the tray," she says, "but you'll need to bring it back tomorrow. Hopefully, my mom won't notice, but it might be best if you bring one of yours next time."

"Well, it won't be me," I say. "But I'll tell whoever you pick next."

She nods, and I think I detect a flicker of uncertainty in her expression, but then it's gone, replaced by a broad smile. "I guess that will depend on when I'm horny."

"So, in ten minutes then," I laugh.

"Sounds about right." She laughs, too, and finds a dishcloth to wrap around the hot tray so I can carry it home.

I look at my watch, conscious that I need to get a move on or I'll be late for my first lecture. Gabriella is probably thinking the same thing, but between my legs, my cock has other ideas.

"Wanna go again," I say, tipping my head to the stairs so Gabriella is clear on my intentions.

"Seriously?" Her wide eyes and raised brows make me smile. I bite my bottom lip at all of her sweetness.

"Seriously."

"You'll ruin me for your brothers," she says. "I won't be able to walk after a repeat of what we did upstairs."

"Maybe we shouldn't, then," I say, already regretting my selflessness.

"There'll be other times," she says softly. "I'll get used to the size of you all, and then it won't be such a big deal."

"I like the sound of that," I say, taking hold of her hands and pulling her toward me. Our kiss is like honey on my tongue, so sugary and delicious I never want it to stop, but as with everything good, there always seems to be a limit. When she pulls back, I bend to kiss her forehead. "This has been…"

There's no word that can encapsulate everything it's been, and when Gabriella nods before I finish my sentence, I know she understands.

"It really has been," she whispers. "I better shower."

"Yeah. I need to head off." I take hold of the tray, breathing in the scent of what will be waiting for me later.

Our hands brush and a crazy wave of static runs over my skin, ending in a shiver at the back of my neck. Gabriella straightens, and I wonder if she felt it too.

"My sneakers are by the front door," I say, and she grins.

"I better take this back then, so you can put them on."

We shuffle the tray between us and I slide my sneakers on as quickly as I can, conscious that Gabriella is holding the hot, heavy tray. When I take it from her, she drops her head to one side. "So, I guess I'll see you around."

"Yeah. You will."

"Bye."

With the food between us, kissing her again would be a challenge, bordering on treacherousness, so I nod as I pass through the door she's opened for me.

And that's how we end the first morning of our deal.

I haven't smiled so much in years.

6

DALTON

"This is delicious," I say, scooping up another huge mouthful of chicken and roasted vegetables and shoving it into my mouth. "Seriously."

"I know, right?" Kain nods, dabbing his mouth with a napkin. "You should see how quickly she rustled it up."

"It's the multitasking I'm impressed by." Blake takes a swig of beer from the condensation-covered bottle and grins. "A woman who can cook and fuck at the same time is like my idea of perfection."

"You sound like a friggin' caveman." Kain grimaces.

"I'm sure Gabriella would love a man who can fuck and change a tire at the same time."

"Or fuck and organize an expensive date," I add.

They both turn to me. "Dating isn't in the deal," Kain reminds me.

"It was hypothetical." I'm quick to deny that my train of thought is taking me anywhere outside our arrangement. Whether they believe me is another matter. My mind may have imagined stepping out with Gabriella on my arm, both of us dressed to the nines, ready for an expensive meal. She's a knockout in sweats and leggings but seeing her in something tight and sexy and getting to treat her to a special evening would be amazing.

I'm getting ahead of myself.

I just need to enjoy the moment. Whenever and whatever the moment might be.

"I can't believe you won't tell us about it," Blake says.

Kain clenches his jaw and lowers his silverware. "I told you that what happens between us and Gabriella separately should stay our own business. Having a big public discussion about it isn't for me. You'll find out what it's like to be with her soon enough. You don't need me spilling the details."

"Did you bust a nut in record time? Is that why you're being so fucking coy?" Blake asks.

"What do you think?" Kain looks between us, his nostrils flaring.

"I'm sure Kain ensured the Nowak name wasn't damaged."

Blake nods, amused as always at our youngest brother's defensiveness and competitiveness. "You must have jerked off like a sixteen-year-old nerd before you went over there."

"Is that your plan?" Kain asks Blake. I won't admit that I've thought about doing it. Draining the weasel seems like a good idea. When I get to enjoy my part of the deal, I want to be able to make an impression. Just recalling the image of Gabriella's pussy sets me off. It was like a sweet pink rose, with soft petals I wanted to run my fingers over.

Shit. I'm glad my brothers can't read my mind. They'd think I'm a complete loser if they could.

I might be the largest of us, but I'm the one with the biggest heart. The softest heart too. At least that's what our mom used to tell me. She said God sent me first because he knew I'd always be kind to my baby brothers.

Sometimes I want to bang their heads together, but I never do because I know she's looking down on us and I want her to see the best in me like she did before she died.

"Don't you worry about me," Blake says.

"His dick has got so many holes in it, he'll probably struggle to get it up," Kain snorts.

"Piercings are all about a woman's pleasure, Kain. Maybe you should think about getting some."

"Anyone who tries to put needles in my junk is going to lose theirs."

It's safe to say that Kain and Blake have very different opinions when it comes to body modification. I'm with Blake on tattoos but Kain on piercings. Let's just say people would die if they came anywhere near my dick with anything remotely sharp.

"So, who's next? Can you tell us that at least?" Blake forks his last bite and tosses his silverware down, leaning back with satisfaction and fixing his gaze on Kain.

"She didn't say. I guess it depends on when she's horny…and she's not going to ask for any of us by name. Just put a message out for whoever is available."

"And leave us to fight it out?" That's a direct challenge if I ever heard one, but I'm used to Blake being that way. He likes to poke and prod us with his humor and see who'll be the first to bite back.

Kain licks over his teeth and drinks what's left of his water, taking his time to reply. "I think we're mature enough to figure out a way to determine who answers the call."

I disagree with that sentiment, but I'm not going to say so. "Maybe it would help to set some parameters so that it's easier to work out. For example, if one of us is available, that's easy. If two of us are available, it should default to whoever didn't go last time."

"And if there's three of us available, like right now?"

I push my plate into the center of the table and rest my arms against the cool wood. The patience I require for my middle brother is way more than my baby brother. Go figure. "Again, it should default to whoever hasn't been the longest."

"Unless she asks for one of us in particular?" Trust Blake to think he's going to deliver the best dick and be number one on Gabriella's speed dial. The guy is way too cocky for his own good, and I know I don't have anything to worry about in that regard.

"Stop trying to suggest you're the best fuck," I snort, tossing my used napkin at his head.

"It's the piercings and my charm. What can I say?" He sticks his tongue out and the metal bar glints.

"We don't all need metal." Kain stands and takes his plate into the kitchen, loading the dishwasher before he begins to wash Darleen's dish. "Whoever is next needs to take this back. And take a big pan or tray so that whatever Gabriella cooks can be brought home."

"This is like the best deal ever," Blake practically sings. "Pussy and dinner. It's like having dessert first."

"Yeah. Working up an appetite too," I add.

"My quads took a pounding today," Kain says. "First with Gabriella and then at training."

"Coach will be on to you if your performance takes a sudden nosedive," Blake warns.

"Don't worry about me. My performance is excellent on both fields of play."

"Thank god Gabriella can't hear us." I shake my head, picking up my phone to check that it'll notify me if a message comes through. Even though we're joking with Kain about his performance, I very much doubt Gabriella will be in need of our services tonight. Then again, what the fuck do I know about her sex drive? She could be a nympho who's permanently attached to that vibrator. I know if I fucked her this morning, I'd be happy to fuck her this afternoon and this evening, too. The word happy doesn't cut it. I'd be ecstatic to fuck her morning, noon, and night for the rest of my damned life.

And that's something I'm not going to admit to my brothers.

Blake rises to deal with his plate, too. "While we're all here, how are we going to explain the food to dad?"

"We could try passing it off as our own?" I suggest.

"Like he's going to believe that?"

"Darleen?"

"No way. He'd want to go round and thank her for her contributions and then we'd be found out."

"How about we say we're paying for a home cooked delivery service?" I suggest. I know there are women who work small businesses from home offering something more wholesome than takeaway. To be honest, I don't know why we didn't come up with this idea sooner.

"That sounds like a plan," Kain agrees.

"So we've got our stories straight and decided who's going and when. I guess I can hit the shower." Blake heads to the door, humming something he must have heard on the radio on the way home.

When he's stamped his way upstairs, and Kain has finished with the dish, he returns to his place at the table, eyeing me carefully. "You really okay with all this, Dalton?"

"Yeah. Why wouldn't I be?"

"I just know how much of a crush you had on Gab before."

I straighten in my seat. "Before what?"

"Before we stopped telling each other about our crushes."

I totally get what he's saying. There was a time, when I

hit sixteen, when I stopped talking about girls with my brothers. At least, stopped confiding the feelings part. I guess Kain is asking me if the way I felt then is the way I feel now. I'm not sure I want to share that with him.

"I'm cool, Kain. Really."

"Good. Okay. You'll tell me if you're not, right?"

"Right." I nod my agreement even though I feel uncomfortable.

My little brother's brow draws down for just a moment, then he presses his big hands to the table and stands. "I hope it's you next," he says before he heads upstairs too.

"Because Blake's such a boastful asshole?"

He shoots me a grin and nods.

And I'm left alone, holding my phone, hoping to God that when that message comes, it is going to be me next.

7

DALTON

The message comes the next day when I'm five minutes from home and covered in sweat and grime from a hard day's work.

Gabriella - I'm in need of some 'eggplant emoji'. Who's gonna give it to me?

I pull over, balancing my phone in my hand, and almost drop it in my haste to respond.

Me - I'll be there in fifteen.

It's the quickest message I've ever sent. My thumbs moved at the speed of lightning. Call me Quick Draw McGraw. Gabriella's quick to respond, too.

Gabriella - See you in fifteen, big boy.

Gabriella - What am I cooking tonight?

Me - Meatball spaghetti.

Gabriella - Sounds good to me.

Blake - Have fun, kids!

Kain - Blake! Seriously, dude. Not cool.

I toss my phone onto the passenger seat, signaling to get back into the flow of traffic, desperate to get home,

with Kain so that it's ready after." Her eyes drift to the door to the hallway like she's already imagining us climbing the stairs. "I can cook first, or after…"

"AFTER." The word comes out like a growl and Gabriella's eyebrows shoot up.

"Alrighty then." Just at that moment, my stomach rumbles and the amusement that tugs at Gab's expression is mortifying. "You hungry in more ways than one, Dalton?"

I take a step closer to her, no longer able to hold back the urge I have to touch her. My hand drifts to her hair, taking a soft strand and running it between my rough fingertips. She's elegant and reserved, and I'm gruff and impatient. I hope the combination will be dynamite.

"This has been a long time coming," I say, noting that the huskiness in my voice increases the closer I get to her.

"It has," she whispers as I rest my hand against her slender neck, feeling the fluttering of her pulse under my palm.

I loom over her like the shadow of a mountain, half afraid that I might break her if I let go of my fingernail grip of restraint, half looking forward to showing her what a man like me can do for her. "You think about this a lot?" I ask.

"Since I was thirteen," she admits.

Shit. I remember those days, feeling her cool blue eyes on me and feeling awkward in my body that had grown too big, too fast. I was halfway to being a man, and she was just a girl, but the connection was there for both of us.

"Tell me what you imagined, and I'll make it happen." I trail my thumb over her lips, the rush of breath she inhales cooling my skin.

"I imagine you pulling me into your lap, controlling my movements even though I'm on top."

Shit. Hearing her fantasy is so damned sexy. Knowing

she's thought about what we're going to do together in the same way I have is almost too much.

The time for talking and soft touches is over.

I palm her ass, lifting her quickly, forcing her legs around my hips. She's light compared to what I'm used to lifting every day as part of my job. I silently thank construction for building me into a man who can handle himself. Gabriella gasps as I bring my mouth to hers and stride into the hallway, beginning my ascent of the stairs.

She tastes like minty toothpaste and smells of something floral that tickles my senses. I go easy because I don't want to give her beard-burn within the first five minutes, but when she moans into my mouth, it's too much. I stop halfway up the stairs, forcing her back to the wall, grinding my thick cock against her pussy and devouring her lips. We're a frenzy of scrambling hands and urgent bodies. My knees feel weak, my cock like it could break through the wall currently propping up Gabriella.

When we draw apart for breath, she laughs in a crazed way. "Shit, Dalton. Bedroom now!"

"Yes, ma'am," I joke, grateful for a moment of lightness and laughter between us, a space in time where I can calm my racing heart.

In Gabriella's room — Planet Angel as we used to call it — I look around at the big bed, the desk stacked with books and papers, the open closet filled with colorful clothes. Her window faces Kain's room, and I realize how easy it would be for them to spy on each other if they wanted to. In the corner, by an overflowing bookcase, is a large blue armchair with worn fabric and a fluffy cream cushion. The perfect place for me to make Gabriella's fantasy come true.

It would be easy for me to sit with her still in my lap, but that isn't what she imagined. I lower her to her feet, relishing how she has to crane her neck to look up at me. I walk slowly to the chair, easing myself into it like a king taking his place on a throne. She watches as I spread my legs and lean back, resting my arm casually across the arm of the chair. Dropping my head to one side, I take a few seconds to absorb the beauty of the woman in front of me. Her dress is ruffled, her hair mussed from my hand. Her lips are swollen and rosy-pink, and her hands hang at her sides. She seems unsure of what to do, but that's okay. I want to lead.

"Take off your dress, Gabi. Show me what you've been hiding under there."

Rather than lifting it over her head, she slides a strap from her shoulder, and then another, gradually leading the fabric downward. She reveals a black satin bra with a shiny diamond at the center and breasts that curve into a nice handful. Lower, a narrow waist widens into curvy hips and satin panties that I want to tear from her with my bare hands. A little jewel glints at her navel and I wonder how Blake will react when he finds out Gab has a piercing too. I run my hand over my beard once, twice, and fold in my lips, imagining what she'll taste like.

It wasn't part of her fantasy, but it is part of mine.

"Come closer," I say, using my index finger to beckon.

Gabriella steps from her dress and pads forward until she's within touching distance.

I hook my fingers into both sides of her underwear, leaning forward to kiss the curve of her soft belly along the line of her panties. Her fingers thread through my hair, setting nerve endings buzzing as I ease my hands down her thighs.

Oh fuck.

I'm so close.

When my fingers touch her ankles, I let go, tapping her inner calf, urging her to widen her stance. I inhale, scenting her arousal, trailing my finger up the inside of her leg until she's trembling and gripping my hair until it's almost painful.

Like the deviant I am, I trail my index finger over her entrance, find her already wet enough to fuck. I part those pretty pink petals, loving the way she squirms against my finger. She's so warm and smooth, and when I find her little clit, it's swollen and ready.

"Shit, Dalton," she gasps.

Before she can utter another word, I grab her ass with both hands and tug her hips until my mouth is on her pussy. The first taste is a hit of dopamine so strong it makes my head spin. I'm so damned hungry for more and push my tongue along the path my finger just made, reaching the place where she's slick and ready and lapping it up. I probe her entrance, feeling it flutter, knowing that just a little deeper inside is that little bundle of nerves that will make her come. If she was on her back on the bed, I could reach it, but like this, it's impossible.

I flick at her clit, once, twice, then use the roughness of my whole tongue until she's panting and writhing and so wet that her inner thighs are damp. With one hand, I push down my shorts, freeing my cock. I have to pull back to tear open the foil packet and Gabriella rests both hands on my shoulder, watching.

"Looks like cock size is a genetic factor," she whispers, with a dance of amusement in her tone.

"Lucky you," I say, leaning back, letting my cock take center stage. And he does. I'm happy to say that I'm totally in proportion.

"Lucky me," she whispers.

It's time for Gabriella to get what she wants.

"Get on here." I reach for her hand, tugging her closer, supporting her weight as she kneels either side of my hips. My hands cup her ass, tugging her. She unfastens her bra, freeing the breasts I've been craving to see bared. Her hair is so long, it hangs like a mermaid's, revealing her nipples and some creamy, soft skin. I push it away, gathering it in one hand and using my grip on it to bring her closer. When I wrap my lips around one tight point, I relish her soft exhale, and deeper moan as I suck hard.

My mind spins with a surge of blood, driven by my racing heart and all the tension gathering in my body. I'm so close to being inside Gabriella, so close to knowing whether my fantasies were anything close to reality. She shifts forward, one hand reaching between us to encircle my cock. There's nothing tentative about the way she touches me, grasping hard and pumping with determination. I have to throw my head back to catch my breath and focus on her touch.

It's too much and not enough all at the same time.

Her wrist is tiny in my big hand, and I squeeze gently, letting her know she needs to stop without having to say the words. "It's time," I growl.

"Dalton…"

We both focus on the space between our bodies, watching as I grasp my cock in one hand and shift her body closer with the other. Her pretty pussy is spread wide, and I stroke through her wetness, coating the end of my cock, making us both hiss with pleasure. "Sit on it," I order, knowing she'll need the ability to move at her own pace. I hate it when guys brag about rearranging a girl's guts, but my cock is so big against Gab that it looks as though it's going to hit her diaphragm.

She bites her bottom lip and frowns, letting my cock press against her little hole. Fuck, this is ridiculous. Impossible. But suddenly, it's not.

Women are miraculous things. Their bodies seem capable of the impossible. As she lowers down on my dick, inch by incredible inch, I can't stop watching her stretching and expanding to take me in.

"Fuck, Dalton. You're such a big boy."

My heart swells and I wrap my arms around Gabriella, wanting her to feel just how into this moment I really am.

8

GABRIELLA

There's a song by SZA called Big Boy and it's been running through my head on a loop since I opened the door to Dalton, and he obliterated the light that should have streamed in from outside with his huge body.

Damn, he's massive. Big hands like shovels. Broad chest and thick arms corded with the muscles of a working man. Dark beard I could get lost in. And his cock? Well, all I can say about that is 'chef's kiss'.

Dalton's not a boy anymore.

That ship has sailed.

He's well and truly a man who's capable of wrecking my comparably tiny body. Right now, I feel like I'm a finger puppet, and Dalton's cock is a giant fist. What's happening between us shouldn't be humanly possible, but somehow my body is making it work.

I can't tell you how grateful I am that he's pushing into the stretchiest part of me, or that he's allowing me complete and total control.

It's a struggle for him to hold back. I can tell by the way he's gripping the arms of the beaten-up old chair that

I love so much, and the way his jaw ticks with restraint.

Shit, that part is sexy.

Dalton is like a large breed dog, all big and strong and friendly, but behind the facade, I know he's a fucking animal. I just hope he's going to let go and show me that part of him. If I can't make him growl like a grizzly, I'm going to feel like a failure.

I drop my head back, letting my hair tickle my lower back, gripping Dalton's inked bicep, using small thrusts to take him deeper. "Fuck," I groan, as my eyes roll. The stretching is so good, so perfect.

Yesterday with Kain flashes through my mind, but it doesn't feel weird to be thinking of another man during sex with Dalton. The Nowaks always do everything together. Somehow it makes this deal we have feel natural even though to anyone else it would be strange and maybe a whole lot of fucked up.

"You're nearly there." Dalton's voice is husky and his hands have moved to grip my hips. In my fantasy, he used me like a rag doll, forcing my body to move over his, demanding what he wanted and making me come like a banshee in the process.

"Make me," I whisper, not wanting to be patient anymore. The tips of his fingers press deeper into my flesh, and he shoves me down until his cock bottoms out. I'm not close to taking him all. I could still wrap my hand around the thick root of his erection if I could reach that far, but that's not what Dalton wants.

What he wants is my slick pussy, clasping whatever he can push inside me. He wants my hands on his chest, grabbing at him in a frenzied, desperate way that seems to make him crazy. I bend to kiss him, managing to keep my mouth on his even as I bob up and down, impaled on his monster-sized cock. In less than a minute, and with no friction on my clit at all, I'm gasping. "Oh…oh…fuck…oh…Dalton…don't…fucking…stop."

And he doesn't. He keeps grabbing at me, shifting my hips, hammering against my G-spot until it's me who's grunting like an animal in heat. I lose control of my limbs, legs going limp, hands slipping from Dalton's skin; a marionette with its strings suddenly severed. Dalton wraps his enormous arms around me, cradling me against his chest. He smells so good, like the forest and sea breeze and sexy, sexy man. His beard scratches my forehead as he presses desperate kisses there. He's still shifting beneath me, letting his cock slide in and out, slowly keeping a rhythm that isn't too much for me. "That's it, baby," he whispers against my skin. "That's it. Let me take care of you."

His rough hands caress my body in long slow strokes, relaxing me and prolonging my blissed-out state. "That feels good," I whisper.

"I know what you need," he says. The words should sound cocky, but they don't. Mostly, he sounds happy at the idea that he can please me. Dalton's awesome with the aftercare that most guys don't seem to have a clue about. His focus hasn't shifted to chasing his own release. His ocean eyes watch me, taking in everything, and I wonder what he's thinking and feeling about this moment.

Is it weird to be buried between the thighs of a girl you used to play tag with in your backyard? Is it weird to touch her tits and lick her pussy, and to know her so intimately?

From my perspective, it isn't weird at all, and I'm not sure how I should feel about it. These men have been a solid and stable part of my life for so long. I've lusted after them for more years than it's probably been good for me. I trust them in a way I've never been able to trust another man. That isn't to say I trust them with my whole heart and soul, but that has more to do with my own hang-ups than the Nowak brothers themselves.

It feels natural to let Dalton pet me gently with his big, rough hands. It feels good to sink against him because I know this means as much to him as it does to me. I remember when I fell on the sidewalk outside our houses, and he picked me up and carried me inside so my mom could tend to my shredded knee. He watched the whole cleanup and bandaging process, biting the side of his nail with as much concern as if I was having my whole leg stitched back on.

I touch his face as the tenderness I felt when I was a clumsy kid rushes back to me with as much force as if it had happened yesterday.

"That was so fucking sexy," he says, kissing the pad of my thumb. Inside me, his cock seems to thicken, an indication that he's ready for his turn now.

"Let me feel you come, Dalton," I say, pressing a kiss to his soft lips, relishing the scratch of his facial hair against my skin.

A growl rumbles in his throat, and as if he can't wait anymore, Dalton starts to thrust upwards. My breasts bounce with every movement, and I have to grip his shoulders to stay upright. "Oh…oh…" I pant, wincing a little as he hits too deep every so often, wanting to weep from how close he's bringing me to coming again.

His eyes are closed, his jaw set, his biceps so bunched that his veins bulge tracks through the skin. The lion on his shoulder seems fiercer, as though it's going to roar at the same time as Dalton growls his release.

"That's it," I say. "Fill me up, baby. Fuck me with that big cock. Fill me…" I don't get to complete the sentence before Dalton swells, jerking into my pussy as though his life depends on it. He unleashes a rumbling groan that can probably be heard from the sidewalk, clutching at my body with fingers that I know will leave bruises in the morning. For all his care, in the moment of ecstasy, his carefulness crumbled, replaced by a frenzy of desire.

"Fuck," he breathes, still pumping his hips, still holding me against him so tightly I can barely inhale. "Fuck, Gabi.

Oh Fuck."

I wrap my arms around his neck, bring our bodies so close that there's not even a paper's width of space between us, and he hugs me tightly too.

When his cock slides out with an audible plop against his belly, he sighs with contentment, and I laugh just a little with happiness.

This deal is going better than I ever could have hoped for. These men know just how to rock my world without shattering my heart. There isn't a single downside to this kind of low-risk sex.

I've never had a fuck buddy before, but that's what my brother's best friends are quickly becoming.

I fiddle with the hair at the back of Dalton's neck, letting him relax. I need to pee, probably because his dick violated my body in the best kind of way. But I'm not going to disturb our post-sex peace. No buzzer is going to go signaling the food is ready like yesterday. There's no pressure for us to move at all.

"My god, girl. You just about killed me." He takes my hand and presses it to his thudding heart. Since the last time I saw Dalton shirtless he's developed a dusting of soft dark hair across his chest that makes me want to purr.

"What a way to go, though, right?"

He laughs, sliding his hands over my thighs and hips, happily exploring the landscape that almost brought about his untimely death. "The best, baby. That would be the best."

I swat his dinner-plate sized pec. "I'm not ready to lose you just yet."

"That's good to hear."

I sigh softly, snuggling into his embrace. It's natural and easy to be this way with him, as though no time has passed since we were lying in the long grass, counting insects and watching the clouds morph into fluffy white shapes. Unlike Kain who was in a rush, I have time to connect with Dalton and I'm going to make the most of it. "What did you think when Kain told you about our little deal?"

"I thought I hit the jackpot, but before that, I wondered if my little brother might have had an aneurysm!"

"And Blake?"

"You know Blake. He's always happy about everything. That guy can see the bright side at midnight."

"He can," I agree, Blake's lopsided smile and sparkling eyes flashing into my mind. "And you aren't jealous of each other?"

Dalton shrugs. "Nowaks are taught to share from an early age. It's a family thing. The threat of my father giving us a good whooping if we didn't was enough to ensure our compliance."

"I think your dad would give you a good whooping if he could see you now."

Dalton nods, blowing out a tight breath. "You're right about that. I don't think your mom would be too happy about the deal either…or Travis."

"Well, they don't need to find out, do they? Kind of makes it more fun to sneak around."

"The forbidden fruit always tastes the sweetest." He nods, agreeing with the sentiment of the phrase, and I stare at him, surprised. Of all the Nowak brothers, Kain always seemed like the most intellectual, with Blake running second. Dalton was the one who was best with his hands. The practical one. He had his heart set on working with his dad from an early age, so I wouldn't have expected him to be so philosophical.

"I like the idea of being forbidden," I whisper, and he slaps my ass affectionately.

"Who would have thought sweet little Gabriella would

grow up to be such a naughty girl?"

"A lot changes with time, doesn't it?"

Dalton nods. His eyes drift to the tattoo on his forearm of his mom when she was in her early twenties. It's almost photo quality and the softness in her eyes reminds me so much of Dalton. "Yeah. Not all for the best."

I know he's talking about his mom, and I suddenly think of my dad; sad changes for two very different reasons.

"What time's your mom back?" he asks.

I look up, forcing myself to remember what day it is and her shift patterns. "Two hours," I say. "I'll make our dinner at the same time I make yours."

"I'll help you," Dalton says. "Maybe you can teach me. We can't be reliant on your charity for too long."

"It's not charity when you're giving me something in return, Dalton."

He raises his eyebrows, dropping his head to one side. "I think we're getting more than our fair share from this deal. You need to come up with something else you want to even things out."

I rub my chin, narrowing my eyes to appear comically thoughtful. "Mmmmm…what else can I ask for?"

"Flowers. Chocolates. Foot rubs."

"Aren't all those things relationship material?"

Dalton shrugs, seemingly not bothered about the idea of taking this deal out of booty call territory and into something more romantic. "How about jewelry?"

"Damn, Dalton. Are you trying to hit top-boyfriend status?"

"You deserve the world, Gabriella."

My breath rushes between my lips. In five words Dalton takes us from joking into throat burning, tear-jerking territory. I swallow down the lump and paste on a bright smile. "Let's go cook you some meatballs and you can decide if the world is enough."

I shift to stand on shaky legs and Dalton holds me by the hips while I let the blood flow back into my cramped limbs. Before I move away to search out something to wear that's suitable for cooking in, he touches the soft curls between my legs. "I like this," he says. "Don't ever wax it away like those women in dirty movies. I hate that prepubescent look. I like a woman to be a woman."

I've never wanted to wax myself into Barbie territory, but I assumed most men would prefer it. It's good to hear that not all men internalize the images they see in porn. If it's possible, his grown-up attitude only makes me like him more.

"Yeah, well you need to keep this too." I touch the soft dusting of hair across his chest and follow the path of his happy trail down his stomach. "I like a man to be a man."

Dalton takes my hand and kisses my fingertips, rising from the chair to loom over me. We dress in a comfortable silence, and as I'm pulling on a shirt, I spot movement in Kain's room through my sheer drapes. My window is open and so is his. Depending on how long he's been home, he might have heard me and Dalton in the throes of passion.

When Dalton's dressed in his shorts and shirt, I open my bedroom door and we both descend the stairs. With every step, it's like real life comes into focus. Pictures of me and Travis line the wall, but I don't focus on them today.

My mom's apron hangs behind the kitchen door, and I'd usually use it, but today it doesn't feel right.

It's only spaghetti and meatballs, but somehow, the very prospect of cooking for the Nowaks is now twisted up in the hottest sex I've ever had.

I'm never going to be able to look at spaghetti and meatballs the same again!

9

DALTON

If someone told me I could find onion chopping sexy, I'd have told them they were crazy, but that's before I had the pleasure of watching Gabriella cook for me.

Her slender fingers handle the knife with an expert quality, chopping everything fast and small. "It's better if the onions are small," she says. "A lot of people don't like them, but you need them to add flavor. This way, they practically disappear into the sauce. Here, you try."

She holds out the knife and I hesitate, knowing my thick fingers are going to struggle to accomplish the same thing. She doesn't back down, though. "You won't learn if you don't try," she says softly.

I take the knife, focusing all my attention on the half-sphere of white onion left on the wooden board. The blade is sharp and cuts without much effort. I go slow, keeping the distance between cuts the same as Gabriella's. "That's it," she says. "You've got it."

When I finish, I hand her the knife again. "It's harder than it looks."

"Everything in life just takes practice," she says. "If you

can build a house, you can make a meal."

I nod, agreeing with her sentiment. My dad always told us that the only difference between successful people and bums was that successful people are prepared to make mistakes, learn, and try again. They aren't put off by challenge and adversity, and usually I'd take this kind of thing in stride. But today's task is laced with two parts that are unsettling. The first is that Gabriella is watching me and the second is that Mom used to make this same dish for us when we were kids. That's probably why Kain bought these ingredients. It used to be his favorite meal. He didn't stop to think about how I would feel watching Gabriella recreate the past in this way.

"Right, you want to put some oil in first and set it to medium heat. You want the onions to cook through but not burn." She shows me how much, and tips the onions in. "You can stir these while I chop the garlic."

We work side by side in a way that feels companionable. My mom and dad didn't have this kind of relationship. He was the grafter, and she was the housewife. They were happy fulfilling their very different roles, but that isn't the kind of relationship I want.

I want this. Working with my woman to create a life together. I want us to have each other's backs through all of our experiences. Dad would probably tell me it's a recipe for disaster. Their generation wanted very clear roles, but our world is different. Most women work now. They can't be expected to still fulfill all the home duties too.

I glance down at Gab, who's chopping three tiny cloves into miniscule pieces. With her long hair tied up in a loose bun and tendrils falling around her face, she's just perfect. "Here," she says, scraping the garlic into the sizzling pan. "Keep stirring. I'll get the meatballs."

She disappears behind the door to the large old fridge that has probably served this family for over twenty years, emerging with the monster packet that Kain provided. My mouth waters and, more embarrassingly, my stomach growls. Gabriella laughs. "Poor Dalton." She touches my arm. "I made you hungry and didn't feed you. Do you want a cookie?"

"I'll wait," I say. "I want to savor this meal."

She nods, smiling, and I stir the pot more vigorously, not wanting anything to catch on the bottom. One by one, Gabriella tosses the meatballs in and they sizzle noisily. "Brown, then all around. Try not to break them up."

"That seems like a lot of responsibility."

"I know you're up to it."

She's cheeky, which is cute. While I'm battling to fry the meat, she's gathering herbs and cans of tomatoes. From the fridge, she snags a half-finished bottle of wine. "Two cans of tomatoes," she says, adding them. "Basil. Salt. Black pepper. A little oregano. Red wine. Oh, and a squeeze of tomato paste. You can turn down the heat now and we're going to leave this to simmer."

It smells amazing.

"Now for the pasta."

"I know what I'm doing with that," I say.

"Okay. Show me."

I fill a big pan with water and salt it like the ocean, setting it to bring it to a rolling boil.

"Perfect," Gabriella says.

"Now the pasta." I add the spaghetti, lowering it slowly so the water doesn't splash.

"Now stir it." She hands me a slotted spoon and I swirl the water, trying to make sure nothing sticks.

As the water boils, the air fills with moisture and Gabriella's hair curls around her face. I touch a strand, mesmerized by her natural beauty. She touches the same place, grimacing.

"It wants to be curly," she says. "I'm always fighting against it."

"Why? Curls are beautiful." I drop my gaze to the apex of her thighs, and she laughs softly.

"You're starting to sound a little obsessed with my pubic hair, Dalton."

"There isn't a man on this street who wouldn't be obsessed with your pubic hair if he had a chance to see it."

"Your dad lives on this street," she says, and wheezes with laughter when I grimace.

"Don't bring Old Man Nowak into our sex talk," I say. "I have to work with that dude, and his ear hair is out of control. The thought of him thinking anything sexual is gross."

"What about Mr. Grady?"

I stuff my fingers into my ears and sing la la la because that's almost worse. The dude must be eighty-five.

Gabriella embraces me, laughing so much she struggles to catch a breath.

I push her arms away, shaking my head. "Don't start with the affection now. I'll get a boner and all this food will burn."

Holding her hands out, palms towards me, she grins. "Okay, D. I'll focus on the food."

"That's good. Perfect."

She begins to assemble a large salad, filled with leftover chicken, sweetcorn, croutons, and olives. It looks delicious and I take mental notes about the quantities and her technique and file away the information for another day. I stir the meatballs in sauce gently just to make sure they're not catching on the bottom. The pasta is still cooking but has swelled to almost twice its original size.

"Time to drain that," she says, peering into the pan.

"Okay." I walk it over to the sink and create a gap

between the glass lid and the pan, allowing the water to spill out slowly. The steam warms my face and settles against my skin. Glancing to the side, I catch Gabriella watching me.

"You're not a total idiot in the kitchen, are you, Dalton?"

"I've watched some cooking programs."

"Really?" Her eyebrows shoot up in an adorably surprised way.

"Yeah."

"So you really want to learn?"

"Sure." When I place the pan back on the stove, Gabriella grabs a spoon and tastes the sauce.

"Mmmmm…that is so good. Now all you need to do is combine."

With a ladle, I begin to move the sauce into the pasta pan, and when both ingredients are combined, I stir it slowly to spread the tomato sauce evenly through.

"Your mom was a good cook, wasn't she?" Gabriella says.

"She was. I have her recipe book in the kitchen at home."

"Maybe we should cook something from there next time?"

I stare at her earnest expression, so unbelievably touched that she'd think of something like that. Mom's lasagna was my favorite, and I've never had one as good since she passed away. If Gabriella could recreate that masterpiece, I know I'll never be able to let her go.

"Okay. That sounds good."

"We should get this into the dish you brought with you so I can tackle the washing up."

"No way. That's my job. You've done more than enough."

Gab beams at me, something as simple as an offer to share the burden of a task lighting her up. In the end, I wash, and she dries, and after, I carry the dinner she helped me make to the front door.

"This was nice," she says softly.

"You're amazing," I say, and she beams again.

"I hope the rest of the Nowaks enjoy their dinner." She leans against the wall, watching as I fasten my sneakers, long legs gleaming, tempting me to throw her over my shoulder and take her back upstairs. But her mom will be home soon.

"They will. I know they will. And I'll see you soon, yeah?"

"You will," she nods.

I want to kiss her goodbye, but the dish is in the way. It doesn't matter though because I know this isn't the last time we're going to spend time alone together. There will be more.

As I stroll toward my house, the urge to whistle with happiness is overwhelming.

10

BLAKE

Two days have passed since Dalton went over to Gabriella's and we're all starting to think she's not going to call again. Kain has checked in with Dalton that their time together was good numerous times, and I've ribbed him continuously that he's put her off Nowaks for life. Then, as I'm leaving work, a text comes through.

Gabriella - Who's free?

I drop my bag on the sidewalk so I can answer.

Me - Me.

Gabriella - When can you get here?

Me - Twenty minutes.

Me - I'll need to shower at yours.

Gabriella - Sounds good.

Shit. Twenty minutes. My dick hardens against the thick denim of my torn black jeans, the piercing shifting.

In my car, I adjust myself, taking a quick look in the mirror. My hair still looks good. Ideally, I would have liked to get ready for Gabriella at home, but Dad is probably already there, and I don't want to raise suspicions.

I'll have to park my car around the corner, just in case.

This whole thing feels a bit like fooling around with a girl in high school. I haven't had to worry about what parents think for a few years now.

I listen to my favorite band, knowing the music will hype me up. It's been a long day and I'm tired, but I'm not missing my chance for my first experience with Gabriella. I've had to watch my two brothers walking around with stupid grins on their faces. I've had to suffer them being the first to take advantage of this deal that Kain brokered with our best friend's little sister. My idea, as I keep reminding him.

As I pull up a few houses down, I grab my bag and lock up my car as fast as I can. I stroll to Gabriella's house, telling myself this is no big deal. I'm no stranger to fucking. I'm no stranger to one-night stands. I know how to work out what a girl likes and give it to her so good she'll always remember me with a smile.

Dalton and Kain might have been filled with trepidation about taking this step with Gabi, but I'm not. She's no shrinking violet. She's had her fair share of sexual experiences, some of which I've heard a little about on the grapevine. Dudes are like that about girls they're not in love with. They like to share the graphic details of their encounters as a way of building up their macho status.

For Gabriella to want this deal, she's proven herself to be sexually confident. And we're the lucky three men who get to build on that.

Part of me wishes that Kain and Dalton shared the details of what went down when they visited the Cross house, but those dudes have chosen to be respectful of Gab's privacy. Seems weird when we're all sharing her, but what the fuck do I know? My brothers both have their own minds, unfortunately.

I ring the bell at Gabriella's house, something I've been doing for more years than I care to count. Inside, there's only a muted yellow glow, and it's completely quiet. When we were kids, this house always seemed filled with life. Funny how things change over time.

Gabriella opens the door, and her pretty shadow-rimmed eyes trail me from head to toe. "Looking good, Blake," she says as I step over the threshold. I drop my bag on the floor and survey the dimly lit hallway.

"Thanks," I say. "You too." She really does. In a soft pink tank and shorts set, Gabriella Cross is as sweet as cotton candy.

"No food today?"

Fuck, I forgot. I could have picked something up on the way, but who's going to think about tomorrow's dinner when they've got Gabriella waiting?

"No food. Just me."

"Okay." She runs her fingers over her long golden hair and gently bites her bottom lip. "Would you like a drink? Have you eaten?"

I'm as hungry as a horse, but I don't want to inconvenience her. "I'll have a beer if you have one?"

"Sure." She pads into the kitchen and takes a bottle of Bud from the fridge.

"You want to take a shower?"

I nod, reaching out for the beer which she's opened using her dad's old bottle opener.

"You can use the bathroom between mine and Travis's room."

The last time I was there, we were exiting after bursting into Gabriella's room. If Travis hadn't asked us to rescue his porn collection, none of this would be happening right now. Funny, the things that can be put into motion with an innocent request for help.

"Okay." I take a long swig of beer, grateful for the cool relief and the spread of it in my stomach.

"I'll take you up."

I follow Gabriella up the stairs, my eyes never leaving her peachy ass as it wiggles with every step. Damn, she's filled out nicely. Curvy in all the right places. Long slender legs that I'm going to relish getting between.

As we get to the top, Travis's door looms. *Forgive me*, I say internally, not wanting to think about what he'd think of me if he knew what I was about to do. The back of my neck feels hot, and I turn away, trying to brush off the guilt.

Gabriella's room smells of flowery perfume and is perfectly tidy except for a spread of books and papers on her desk. Before I can take in my surroundings, she opens her closet and pulls out a large white towel. "You can use any products there," she says.

"I won't be long."

"It's fine," she says, shrugging. "I'll tidy up."

There doesn't seem much out of place, but whatever. If Gabriella likes her room Stepford-Wife clean, that's her business.

I make my way into the shared bathroom, looking around at the familiar space, finding it smaller than I remember. I've lost count of the number of times I've messed around in this bathroom. Mostly, after getting dirty in the yard, and before Darleen fed us with something delicious. Sometimes, we'd splash each other with water, and make a mess that poor Darleen must have cleaned up. For sleepovers, we'd clean our teeth, all four of us in a row. Sometimes five if Gabriella wanted to join in and Travis didn't tell her to get lost.

Those were fun times.

I undress and step into the shower, letting the warm water wash away the stresses of the day, and find a bottle of something that smells fruity and scrub myself clean. I think about Gabriella in this shower, naked, her wet hair trailing over her body, her long legs stretching to places I've only been lucky enough to get a glimpse of. My cock thickens under my palm, the piercing at the top sliding between my fingers. Is she going to like it or worry about it? It can go either way.

Well, until it does its job. Then she's going to love it.

I don't linger under the water, knowing I have something way more important waiting for me on the other side of the door. There's no point in getting dressed either. I just wrap the towel around my waist and saunter out, knowing the ink I've covered my body with since we were kids is going to make an impact.

It does. Gabriella's lips part and she stands slowly. "Shit, Blake." When she's close enough to touch me, she lets her fingers trail the black lines of the tattoos I've designed; across my chest, over my shoulder, down my arm and up my neck.

"They're beautiful," she whispers, her pretty eyes flicking to meet mine. "It must have hurt."

"Nothing worth having comes without pain," I tell her. She bites her bottom lip, thinking through my words.

"There are many different types of pain."

She's right. There are. But all of them need to be processed or they scar over, leaving trauma behind.

"I promise I'll only inflict the good kind." I grin, touching her face, the softness of her skin making me sigh. I've touched her cheek like this once before, when we camped out in our backyard and Gabriella fell asleep next to me. We were young, but I remember the rush of protective feelings I had for her. I remember the way her beauty made my heart ache.

"I'll hold you to that," she says. Seconds tick past, the air lingering between us feeling thick and paralyzing. I want to kiss her so badly but to do it, I feel like I need to climb a mountain. This is little Gabriella, the girl who always wanted me to play with her Barbies, the girl who'd tag along to play war games, even though I could tell she hated them. She just wanted to be a part of the fun, a part of our group.

A nagging thought taps the back of my mind. Has Gabriella made this deal because she's still searching for that connection and sense of belonging? When she reaches out and touches my face, my heart skitters in my chest. I know I'm always the joker, the one who strives to focus on the bright side of life. I'm the one who tries not to take things too seriously. The one who suggested this idea in the first place. But I'm also the one who can read people the best. My brothers don't see what I see. It's like they exist on a more surface plane.

"Are you sure about this?" I murmur, turning my face into her palm and kissing the center.

"Yes," she says softly.

"Because, if you're not sure, we can just hang out. I could put on some clothes, and we could watch a movie. Eat popcorn. You know. Just like old times."

Her fingers find the corner of the towel where it is tucked securely. "I'm sure, Blake. But thanks for checking."

Before I can respond, she tugs the towel open, letting it drop to the floor. Her eyes hold mine and a pretty flush spreads across her cheeks. My cock is erect between us, jutting out so far, it's almost touching her, but she resists looking.

Fuck.

This girl is so sexy. Confidence like this is exactly what floats my boat.

"I'm naked, Gabriella," I whisper.

"Yes, Blake."

"I think it's time to get you naked too."

I touch the hem of her shirt, finding the fabric soft and warm. "Need some help?"

She nods, still holding my gaze, and it feels like we're in a competition to see who will break first.

It'll be me. I know it will be. As soon as I get these clothes off Gabriella's body, she's going to be on her back in a flash.

She doesn't resist when I lift the shirt, and she grins when my eyes widen, taking in her naked breasts beneath. They're perfect handfuls, tipped by tight little nipples that make my mouth water. Gabriella doesn't wait for me to remove her shorts, she simply pushes at the fabric on her hips, and they drop to the floor, leaving her totally naked.

In the face of so much perfection, I can't hold on to my restraint any longer. I take a step forward, holding her gaze, my jaw ticking as I grit my teeth. She takes a step back, keeping the distance between us the same, eyes still focused on my face, hands hanging at her sides.

Another step and we're closer to the bed, another and the backs of her legs hit the mattress. "It's pointless moving away from me," I say, my voice becoming husky with want.

"Isn't the chase half the fun?" she says.

I take hold of her hand, bringing the open palm to my dick, forcing her to encircle the rigid bar of my arousal. Her lips part as I rub my piercing against her skin, and finally, she gives in and looks down.

"Oh my god, Blake. You pierced your dick?"

"I did."

"Will it…?"

"Rock your world," I interrupt. "Yes. It will."

"I was going to say hurt me," she says, touching the piercing with the tips of her fingers, stimulating my cock in the most tentatively mind-blowing way.

"No pain, Gab. Just pleasure."

"What about condoms?"

I drop my head to one side, touching Gabriella's cheek. "I can use one, but I won't come inside you in case it tears."

"That can happen?"

"There's a risk, but I know what I'm doing. I can feel it if it happens."

"I'm not on birth control," she says softly. "My mom doesn't think it's a good idea to mess with hormones if you don't need to."

"She's probably right," I say, sliding my hand to the back of her neck where it's warm. "You know I'll take care of you, right?"

She nods, gazing up at me with wide emerald eyes that always had a way of bewitching me, even before I understood the power that women can have over men.

"Can I kiss you now?"

Gabriella nods, and her eyes drift closed with anticipation. For a couple of seconds, I stare down at her peaceful expression, taking in the soft dusting of freckles across her nose, and the long sweep of her darkened eyelashes as they cast shadows over her high cheekbones.

When our lips meet, I don't initially feel a rush of possession and desire. There's something else between us first. A recognition, maybe, of a connection that's been beneath the surface for years. The feeling of coming home.

But when her tongue touches mine, all the soft warmth slips away and, in its place comes a rush of overwhelming need. I hold her, lowering us both to the bed so she's splayed beneath me and I'm looming over her. We don't stop kissing, but now I get to feel her writhing beneath me. "There's no rush," I whisper against the skin of her neck over the place her pulse thuds fast beneath. "We can take our time."

To illustrate my point, I kiss slowly over her body, purposefully missing the parts she really wants me to focus on. Gabriella's fingernails dig into my shoulders as she tries to urge me closer to her pretty pussy.

Before we get to all the good stuff, I want to make sure I know what she needs from me. I want to rock her world at least as much as my brothers, if not more. "Tell me your fantasy," I say. "If you could choose a way for me to fuck you, what would you choose?"

Just as she's about to answer, music begins to play, sounding through Gabriella's window which is thrown wide to let the cool evening air inside. She twists, looking at the window. "Kain," she whispers, the longing in her voice obvious.

I forget his room faces hers. I forget that you can see and hear everything that's going on in the Cross house from his window.

"He's home," I say softly.

Gabriella nods, biting her bottom lip, her eyes staring off to the side as though she's trying to muddle through options.

"What is it?" I ask. "Do you want us to stop because he's there? He knows I'm here, right? He knows because he set this whole thing up with you."

Gabriella tightens her legs around me. "I don't want us to stop…" Hesitating again, she blows out a tight breath.

"Whatever you need, Gab. Whatever you want, I'll give it to you. You don't have to hold your desires inside. Just ask, please?"

"Sometimes I see Kain undressing," she says softly. "Sometimes, I watch him through the drapes. I think he knows."

"Oh, he knows," I laugh. "Why do you think he's always wandering around naked with the light on and the curtains open?"

She laughs and I can feel her body soften beneath mine. "I thought maybe we could return the favor."

"You want him to watch us fuck?" I ask, the idea already causing a rush of blood to my cock. So much that my head spins.

"I want him to see you please me…see you own me."

"You want to make him jealous?" The idea fascinates me because that's not what this deal is about. We're cool with each other because there's never been a time when Gabriella wasn't on all our minds. And from what Travis told me about Gabriella's diary, she couldn't choose between us either.

"Not jealous," she says. "I just want him worked up and wanting."

"Ah…you want to drive him crazy?"

She nods, a wicked little glint making her eyes sparkle. "I want to drive you all crazy."

"And I don't think you'll find a single one of us that isn't unbelievably happy about that," I admit.

"So, you'll do it."

I shrug, grinding my cock against her pussy, making us both moan in the process. "I'll do anything you want, baby. Any fantasy. Anything."

Gabriella's eyes light up even more, and I get the feeling she's already thinking about other things she wants from us. This deal just gets better and better. She swats my shoulder. "We'll need to stand."

That's my favorite way to fuck.

I get to my feet and hold out my hand, helping up a flushed and very naked Gabriella. She makes her way to the window, parting the drapes and staring into Kain's room. I can't see him, but his light is on, and the flickering TV casts colored shadows across his white walls. His window is open too, and the faint murmur of TV voices travels across the narrow divide between houses.

Gabriella grips the windowsill, arching her back so her spectacular ass is raised. I slide my hands from her ribs to her hips, kissing her between her shoulder blades. When she turns to look over her shoulder, I capture her mouth with mine. My dick slides between her thighs, finding her slick and warm. Oh god, I need to get inside her. She's ready and I've barely touched her.

Reaching around, I find her clit, and rub in slow circles while I explore her mouth. Her hand clasps the side of my face, and she moans, rocking her hips against my hand, seeking more pressure.

"I want to taste you," I say.

"Later," she whispers. "Fuck me first."

I reach down to grab the leg of my discarded jeans, finding the condom in the back pocket. I'm careful when I roll it over my piercing, adjusting as I ease it down to the root. When I look up, I notice Kain walk past his window and glance over. Even from this distance, I can see the moment his eyes register Gabriella standing at the window with bared breasts.

He pauses, lips parting, and as I step forward, I feel his moment of realization as vividly as if it were my own.

Taking Gabriella's hair, I move it so it all falls over one shoulder. I put my hand on her belly, pushing so that her back is arched enough for me to access her pussy from behind. She moans when I slide through her labia, my piercing stroking her clit. When I notch at her entrance, I look up to where my brother is watching, and I smile.

Then I shift my hips with as much force as I can muster and bury myself deep in one thrust. Gabriella gasps as her inner walls stretch to accommodate me. Kain reaches for the window frame, the sight of Gabriella's pleasure overwhelming. I bring one hand to her throat and the other to her hip. Like this, I can control the position of her body and her movements. I can show Kain that I'm possessing the girl I know he likes way more than he lets on.

I fuck Gabriella just the way I know she needs, keeping an even rhythm, letting my piercing graze against her G-spot over and over.

"Oh fuck," she moans, her head dropping forward, no longer able to hold eye contact with Kain.

"You gonna come, baby?" I ask, feeling her pussy drawing tighter, knowing it'll be soon.

"Yes," she almost shouts. "Yes, yes, yes."

And I know I've got her right where I want her.

11

GABRIELLA

"Yes," I gasp, no longer able to contain the well of pleasure building inside me. I'm losing control of my physical form, the strange and magical pressure of the metal stud through the end of Blake's cock hitting in a way that I've never experienced before.

"That's it," he says, working his powerful body behind me. I wish I could see his face, but I don't need to know he's enjoying himself. It's there in the slight smugness in his tone, and the way he's moving his hips like a dance he's perfected with years of practice.

His hand moves from my hip to the window ledge, the inky tattooed lines stretching down his powerful forearm and over his fingers. I didn't know that tattoos would set my world on fire. I've always thought of them as tacky, but on Blake and Dalton, they're fire.

I no longer have the strength to keep my head up, such is the coiling pressure in my belly. In the darkness behind my eyelids, my mind plays on a loop of filthy images; Kain licking between my thighs, Dalton's cock spreading my pussy wider than it's ever been spread before, and Blake's dangerously lean body stretched over the top of me.

Three men. Brothers who are similar in so many ways, but immensely different too.

"He's watching," Blake says. "He can't take his eyes off you."

I rest my hand next to Blake's, using the ledge to lever myself back to standing straight, fixing my eyes on Kain again.

"Don't stop," I grunt, gritting my teeth like a wolf who's spotted danger on the horizon. What's building between my thighs feels menacing and savage. A threat so big I might splinter apart with its force.

"Never," Blake hisses, his hips keeping the punishing rhythm that is going to fracture my very soul.

"Oh god. Oh…yes…yes…yes," I gasp. As my knees give way, Blake hooks his arm around my middle, holding me tight. I can hardly breathe, and my heart is practically pounding its way through my ribs.

"That's it, Gab. That's it. Show Kain how good I can fuck you. Show him how amazing I've made you feel."

"Oh, yeah…" My voice is wispy, stolen by the crazy surge of pleasure. All I want to do is collapse on the bed and drift off into the ether, but Blake isn't done, and Kain is still watching. I need to feel the powerful man behind me come. With the amazing piercing in his cock, I get the feeling it's going to be an unusual experience. "Show Kain how good it feels," I order. "Show him what he's missing."

Oh shit. That was really a red rag to a bull.

Blake doesn't need any more encouragement. His fingers bruise my hips, his cock pounds into me beyond comfort. I grit my teeth, determined to take it all, desperate to give him the reward he deserves. "Harder," I order, as my knuckles turn white from the intensity of the grip I need to absorb the ferocity of his thrusts.

"Shit," he hisses, pulling out of me suddenly. His fist nudges into my back as he finishes himself off, removing the condom so he can come over my ass. I turn quickly, witnessing the flush of his release, taking in his glistening chest and taut muscles.

It's a moment of pure surrender from a man who doesn't look like he's capable of letting his guard down. Blake is usually made up of sharp edges, dark ink, hardened muscle, and a wicked smile. Now, he seems dazed, as though he can't believe what's happened.

It's hard for me to take it in, too.

My brother's best friends, the boys I loved when I was a kid, the men I lusted after for years, have all been inside me. They've given me pleasure that surpasses what any other man has ever been able to achieve by miles, and in different ways that fulfill my fantasies.

I totally get why Ellie fell for her stepbrothers in this situation. Three men tick so many more boxes than one man ever could.

But this situation is different, isn't it?

How? My mind whispers in a way I can't ignore as I touch Blake's heaving shoulders. He blinks his eyes that are usually pale as polished silver, but are now almost entirely obliterated by dark pupils, blown wide with arousal.

"Fuck, Gabriella," he mutters as the hand still cupping his cock stills. "That was…"

"Yeah," I say. "It really was. You Nowaks really know how to rock a girl's world."

"That's good to know my brothers haven't been letting the side down."

"Not at all."

I reach down to pick up my clothing so I can dress, but Blake makes a soft tutting noise. "There's no way you're covering up all this goodness right now." His hands skim the air on either side of my body, making exaggerated curvy shapes. "After all that, I want some cuddle time."

"Cuddle time?" I raise my eyebrows, surprised that big, tough, tattooed Blake is such a softy. If any one of the brothers was going to ask for affection time after sex, I would have expected it to be Dalton.

"Yeah. You know. The chill relaxing part after sex. Did my brothers not handle that part?"

I shrug and purse my lips. "To be fair to them, Kain's time was interrupted by the kitchen timer, and Dalton had a short window before my mom was going to be home."

Blake jumps onto the bed, bouncing comically on his knees. "Guess I got the best slot."

Holding his hand out, he beams like an overgrown kid reaching for an adult-sized ice cream.

I climb next to him, and he hooks me with his big arm, settling my head in the nook of his shoulder. His skin is so warm, fragranced with my shower products and etched with intricate swirls of black. I follow them with my fingers, and watch as goosebumps break out in their wake.

"This is nice," he says softly. "A little weird, too."

I know what he means, but I still ask "Why?"

"I remember sneaking into your room when we were kids. Sometimes you'd be happy to see us, and sometimes you'd scream, remember?"

"I was always happy to see you," I say softly. "I just wasn't always up for dealing with the bullshit Travis tended to encourage."

"Yeah. He had a thing for annoying you," Blake admits. "But he was always watching out for you. I guess that's a sibling bond."

"Maybe," I say. "He hasn't called me since he left for Germany. The bond has taken a bit of a beating."

"He loves you," Blake says firmly, squeezing me closer. "He's just overwhelmed with his new life."

"Would you call your brothers if you were overseas?"

"Depends what I was doing and when I was planning on coming home."

"Seriously." I look up, finding him staring up at my cracked ceiling. "You guys have always been thick as thieves. I can't imagine a time when you weren't living in each other's pockets."

"Yeah. I know what you mean. Some of our friends think we're weird."

I frown, shifting so I'm closer to his face and I can get a better view of his expressions.

"In what way?"

"Just that we're so close." He shrugs his other shoulder. "I mean, if we told people about this deal with you, they'd most likely think we were freaks, and not the sexy kind!"

"Even after the Ellie, Colby, Micky, and Seb situation?"

"Yeah. One group love situation doesn't break the prejudice."

"I guess."

"Anyway, you don't have to worry about that. We won't tell anyone about the deal. It's just between us." When Blake presses a soft kiss to my forehead and strokes his thumb over my cheek, I believe what he says. It's not that I'm ashamed about what we're doing. Not really. I've never been the kind of girl to have hang-ups about sex and relationships. It's just that the more people who know, the more likely it is that Travis will find out.

With my mind drifting, I glance down, finding Blake's cock is hard and his piercing is *there*. I just have to ask about it.

"What made you want to do that to yourself?"

He laughs, a full-bellied chuckle that makes me giggle too. "You make it sound like I signed up to torture myself."

"Didn't you? I mean, I can't imagine that someone made a hole through your cock without it causing any pain."

"It hurt but the pain doesn't last. The wound heals over and what's left is worth it. Haven't you ever thought about getting some ink or more piercings?" He touches my earlobe where my tiny diamond studs are glinting and trails his finger to my navel, swirling around the jeweled stud.

"I've thought about getting a tattoo, but my mom wouldn't be happy."

"You're a big girl now, Gabriella. You're going to do lots of things that your mom isn't happy about." He grins, taking my hand and pressing it around his hardening cock to perfectly illustrate his point.

"I was thinking about getting something here." I show Blake the space on my hip that would be covered by most underwear and swimwear.

He trails his fingers over the soft skin there, assessing. "You could have something really nice here. Birds. Butterflies. Flowers. They'll all work to fill the space."

"What about an angel?" I ask.

"Yeah. An angel could work. Maybe a sleeping angel, wrapped in its wings."

I never thought of that before, but that could be exactly the idea that would be perfect.

"Could you draw me something?" I ask him. "I'd like to see your ideas."

"You want me to be the one to do something to your body that your mom would go ballistic over?"

"I think you already did that," I laugh. I kiss his concerned grimace and slowly, our mouths start to move in a synchronized way that flicks all my switches back on to go. We have time for more, I think. Time for it to be less frenzied and kinky and more about discovery. I'm hungry to find out what that piercing will feel like in my mouth and to know what other skills Blake has to show me.

Instead of cooking another meal, I make a meal of Blake and he makes a meal out of me. And it's perfect.

12

KAIN

Coach has a hard-on to hurt us today. Instead of our usual grueling training, he's testing out some new techniques which have left my muscles screaming and my whole body covered with sweat. I glance around at my teammates, finding ruddy cheeks, filthy training gear, and broken spirits.

All training is good for us, especially the kind that pushes us outside comfortable boundaries, but when we're all tired beyond capacity, it doesn't feel positive.

"Fuck," Dornan grumbles. "If Coach doesn't sort out his marital problems soon, I swear I'm going to need to get involved. Maybe we could pitch in and send his wife a big bunch of flowers and some chocolates. Maybe that would do the trick."

"You seriously think he's taking out his marital issues on us?"

Dornan grimaces, running his shovel hands through his disheveled hair. "I don't think it, I know it. I heard him on the phone the other day taking an absolute grilling from his Mrs. He's in the doghouse for sure!"

"That's the side of relationships I can't fucking stand," I say. We start to make our way towards the locker room, following our other lumbering teammates. There's been a different dynamic since a load of men left at the end of last year. Getting used to the newbies and becoming one of the old-timers feels weird. One more year and I'll be done with this, but I'm still not certain what I want to do next.

"You with anyone right now?" Dornan asks.

I turn my head to catch his expression and find the corner of his mouth pulled up in a small grin. It's the kind of grin that tells me he knows something, but he's not saying. Ellie and Dornan are best friends and Ellie is also friends with Gabriella. There could have been a chain of information flow between them all.

"Not with anyone," I say.

Dornan nods, making a very fake interested noise which vibrates my nerves. I'm too tired to mess around with this bullshit. If he has something to say, he needs to just come out and say it.

"You want to play games like a girl, Dornan? Or just come out with whatever you've got balancing on the tip of your tongue."

"I may have heard that Ellie has been flipping the dares Gabriella's way. And that you and your brothers might have been the subject of the dares."

"Dares?" This is new to me. I thought Gabriella agreed to the deal because it was what she wanted, not because of a stupid game she was playing with her friend. My stomach twists with discomfort, the memory of our morning together suddenly colored differently in my mind.

"It's just a stupid game. I used to play it with Ellie. When I knew she wanted something but wasn't brave enough or motivated enough to go after it, I'd dare her. It was a way of encouraging her to live her best life."

"So that's what Ellie is doing for Gabriella?"

"Most likely." He studies me as he holds the door open for me to pass through first. "Ellie's not a bitch. She wouldn't encourage Gabriella to do something she didn't want to do, and Gabriella is pretty headstrong."

"You can say that again," I mutter.

"So, you guys are banging?" Dornan's grin is so mischievous that I can't be mad at him for asking very personal questions. If the subject of his interrogation was anyone other than Gab, I wouldn't care about spilling all the gory details, but I want to protect her from the locker-room gossip if I can.

"Dude. She's a good friend of mine. Even if I was, I wouldn't share it with you."

Dornan nods, still smiling. "What about your brothers? Are they as good as you at keeping secrets?"

Blake can be a blabbermouth, but I'm not about to tell Dornan that. Dalton doesn't mean to share other people's secrets, but he's easy to trick into revealing something he doesn't intend to make public.

"We would all defend Gabriella's honor," I say simply.

Around the locker room, I catch snippets of conversation, mostly about how sore and hungry everyone is. I wish we had a batch of Gab's delicious food at home, but everything she's made so far has been demolished in one sitting.

Dornan nods, pressing his lips together. "Good on you," he says. "With Ellie hooked up and now Gab…maybe it's time I thought about gathering myself a weird harem living arrangement."

I roll my eyes because I didn't confirm anything and he's leaping to conclusions. "You really think you could live like Colby and his brothers do with Ellie?"

He shrugs, tossing a towel over his shoulder. "Love can make even the craziest situation feel normal. At least, that's what Ellie says."

"I guess. But it can't be without sacrifices."

Dornan slams his locker. "Maybe. Or maybe it comes with perks. There's a lot of pressure on men these days. It's not easy to carry the financial burden of a family, especially if your partner wants to stay home for the kids. Everyone seems to be working themselves into divorce. It's too much stress. Imagine sharing that with two other guys. Imagine all the chores in a household split four ways instead of two. Imagine having two buddies to hang out with all the time, as well as a beautiful woman. It kind of sounds perfect to me."

"You are really selling it, Dornan." I chew my cheek, realizing what he's saying is a perspective I never considered. He hasn't even considered the complexity of sharing a sexual relationship. Maybe that part doesn't bother him at all.

Does it bother me? I'm willing to share Gabriella with my brothers as part of our current deal. The boundaries we're working within paint everything a different color. But without those boundaries, could I imagine knowing my girl was fucking someone else? Could I find a way to watch that and not want to tear down walls, brick by miserable brick?

I'm not a jealous man, but I think Ellie's situation could drive me to distraction.

"Gabriella's a good girl," Dornan says. "Whether or not you guys are bumping uglies, just make sure you're decent to her."

"Dude. Bumping uglies has gotta be the worst fucking way to describe sex."

"That's what you're focusing on from what I said?" He rolls his eyes, starting towards the showers.

I stay behind, taking my time finding what I need in my bag. I like Dornan, but I don't need him to tell me what Gabriella needs or deserves. Right now, that's my responsibility.

By the time I'm showered and ready for home, my brain feels frazzled from working through all the pros and cons of a relationship with Gabriella, one that isn't even an option, anyway.

I know one thing for sure. I won't be sharing any of this with my brothers.

13

GABRIELLA

I owe Kain, Blake, and Dalton a meal, but I've been so busy with assignments that I haven't had time to indulge in any more dial-a-dick. That, and my mom has been home more than normal.

"What do you want me to cook tonight?" Mom asks, her face illuminated by the refrigerator light.

I turn off the TV and toss the remote onto the couch next to me. "I don't mind."

I pick at the hole in my jeans, easing a single thread between my fingers, dwelling on the fact that I've missed the Nowak brothers a little too much for comfort.

You miss their dicks, I tell myself. It's okay to miss dicks and mouths and fingers. It's okay to be pining for rock-hard bodies. But I'm not going to get any dick tonight. Not with Mom around. Or am I?

I grab my phone and pull up the group chat that's supposed to be my portal into pleasure.

Gabriella - I'm so damned horny, but my mom is home.

In seconds, I can see Kain is typing.

Kain - You could come here?

I nibble the side of my finger, trying to think through what going to the Nowaks' might mean. Firstly, I'd have to make an excuse to get out of the house. That can be achieved with some planning. Secondly, I don't know who's at home and what that will mean. If all three brothers are there, what would they expect? Could I handle them all one after the other? Bed-hopping sounds fun, but when you're dealing with men with such huge appendages, it involves more challenges. Would they expect something more?

Ellie hasn't confided much about her sex life, but she did confirm that they all sleep in the same bed and sex can be one-on-one or group. The group idea initially struck me as strange. I couldn't imagine a reason why three brothers would want to watch each other having sex. They'd have to take turns, surely, and the waiting around couldn't be that sexy, could it? Then I decided to take a look at some websites and my assumptions were smashed in spectacular fashion. Group sex with three men and one woman is hot to watch, and no one ever needs to stand around watching. There's more than enough to keep all four parties involved.

But am I ready for that? And would Dalton, Blake, and Kain even want to do that?

I recall the original messages sent on our dial-a-dick chat. This is about my fantasies. The Nowak brothers agreed to give me whatever I wanted. If I ask for this, will it be a step too far?

I'm taking too long to reply, and Kain starts typing.

Kain - we could get a motel room. Molly's?

I make a huffing sound because that's where Ellie had her first group rendezvous with her stepbrothers. It's a dump but I don't think any of us would be fixated on the run-down decor.

There's something about the idea of going to a new place specifically for sex that sends heat between my thighs. I could wear my red lace Basque set and my long beige coat. If we're going to do the tacky motel thing, we might as well go the whole hog.

Blake - Come here, Gab. We're waiting.

Dalton - Hell yeah.

Gabriella - I've got to eat first.

Blake - Then we'll eat you!

Dalton - Dude!

Blake - What? We so will!

Kain - He's right, Gab. We're waiting.

Gab - This is starting to feel less like dial-a-dick and more like SMS-for-pussy.

Blake - I can change the name of the chat. That sounds like an improvement.

Kain - No, you can't, Blake. See you soon, Gab x

I drop my phone to the couch, stifling my broad smile for fear that Mom will see. When I look up, she's watching me. "Who was that on the phone?"

"Ellie," I blurt.

"Oh really. It's Ellie who has made your cheeks flame? Do you think I was born yesterday?"

I shrug, not prepared to admit to anything. "Can we just have grilled cheese and tomato soup tonight?" I ask, not wanting to waste time while Mom cooks up her usual storm.

"Sure," Mom says.

I help her gather the butter and cheese from the fridge and she cuts slices of homemade bread for the grilled cheese. I search out a can of tomato soup before Mom can think about roasting her own tomatoes with garlic. There are three men waiting for sex less than twenty feet away.

And I'm now so horny I can barely concentrate.

Mom asks me some questions about Uni, and I ask her about work. We laugh and eat and I'm filled with warm feelings that come with having a happy home. It's a home that started with four of us, and then went down to three, and now it's just two. For a second, I picture Mom in this kitchen with only herself to cook for, and it makes my heart sink. I wish she'd find a good man to live out her days with companionship. I want her to be happy.

"Have you ever thought about dating again?" I ask. It's been over ten years since Dad died and I've never asked her if it's something she'd be interested in.

Her face falls, and I immediately feel terrible. Is it still too much of a sore subject for her to consider? I've seen the grief fade over the years, but maybe she's just gotten better at covering it up. "I'm so busy," she says, glancing out of the window. It's as though she doesn't want to look me in the eye.

"I know, Mom. You work so hard. I see it, but that shouldn't mean you don't have time for friendship and companionship."

"Thanks, sweetie," she says, then changes the subject to her latest conversation with Travis.

After we've finished eating, I load the dishwasher, and then tell her, as nonchalantly as possible, that I'm popping over to Celine's house. Relationship drama is the excuse I give.

"Okay, honey." She smiles, and my belly is filled with sadness at her attempt to cover up what I perceive as enforced loneliness. That and butterflies from the guilt of lying. "I'm not going to wait up. I've got an early shift tomorrow."

"Okay, I'll see you tomorrow."

I run upstairs, thankful that I showered when I returned from college. I slip on a sexy black lace underwear set and throw my favorite sweats over the top. White sneakers finish the casual look. Tossing my phone in my purse, I jog back down, calling out a goodbye as I leave.

The night air is refreshing, but I don't get a chance to enjoy it because I have to move my damned car. I park around the corner, and set off back to the Nowak house, praying my mom isn't looking out the window as I pass home.

It's been ages since I last approached the blue door and rang the bell, and I'm suddenly transported back in time to when I was level with the shiny chrome doorknob. So much has changed since then.

Kain opens the door, standing far back enough that I can enter. I stare around at the home that is still so familiar. The same photos grace the walls, the same hardwood stretches into the den and beyond. The same furniture rests comfortably in the places I remember. It's like a museum to a past life, one where Sofie Nowak, Kain's mom, is still alive, and I'm just a bratty little girl wanting to play with the mischievous neighbors.

"This is so weird," I gasp. "Nothing's changed." I bite my lip when I realize how thoughtless I sound. Of course something's changed. Kain's mom isn't here anymore.

"We never get round to decorating," Kain says.

I wonder if that's true or if he's covering up the grief his father and brothers feel, not wanting to step out of the shadow of the past like my mom.

"It's nice…familiar…"

"Tired looking," he corrects.

Dalton appears from the direction of the kitchen and Blake at the top of the stairs.

Three huge men who seem even larger when they're together.

Damn.

As I look them over, taking in broad chests, muscular arms and thick thighs, I'm not so confident that I can handle this anymore.

14

BLAKE

Gabriella looks like a rabbit caught in the headlights of a juggernaut, and I don't blame her. She's one average-sized woman and we are three large, looming men.

We've set up the broad outline for this deal between us, but as far as I know, we've never actually dealt with tonight's situation.

We're all home.

And Gabriella's in our territory.

Three hungry wolves and one unsuspecting Little Red Riding Hood.

We really are going to eat her all up.

"Would you like a drink?" Kain asks. Good idea. She could use a double vodka to loosen up for what might be coming.

Obviously, everything that happens will be based on her fantasies and with her consent. This deal is for Gabriella, and we're just happy to be along for the ride. But I'm hopeful she might have something specific in mind for tonight, something involving all three of us.

"Let's raid Dad's liquor cabinet," I say, jogging down

the stairs before anyone can disagree. I grab a bottle of vodka, whisky, and some rum that I think he bought on a trip to Jamaica with Mom. Wielding them like a pro, I head to the kitchen, resting the bottles on the countertop so that I can search out glasses and mixers.

"What would you like, Gab?" I ask.

"Vodka and coke," she says softly. Fuck, she looks good. I pour a double measure of vodka and slowly fill the glass with bubbling Pepsi, which is all we have.

When I hand it to her, she takes three long gulps and licks her lips, letting out a breath that sounds nervous. I don't feel the same, but I like the warm spread of alcohol down my throat and into my belly. I enjoy the softening of my mind that comes from having a drink. I tend to get lost in my racing thoughts, but I don't want to do that tonight. I want to focus on Gab. I want to deliver what she wants.

Dalton has a shot of whisky. Kain abstains because his training schedule doesn't leave room for hangovers. I make rum and coke, and down it in record speed.

Who knows how long we've got before Dad returns. Maybe a couple of hours. That leaves no time to nurse drinks like we're at a neighborhood social.

Gabriella's eyes dart around the kitchen, avoiding all of us and fixating on things like the copper pots hanging on the wall and the weird, colorful flat basket that Mom brought from Greece.

Someone needs to deal with the elephant in the room before it gets any more awkward.

"So, Gab. How do you want to play this?" I ask, dropping my head to one side so I can study her reactions. There's a risk that in this pressured situation, she might conceal her true feelings. "Do you want just one of us tonight? That would be Kain, as the current schedule stands." It sounds weird describing our deal in this way, but we might as well be upfront. "Or all of us, one at a time. Or all of us together. We're down for whatever your fantasy is."

She blinks her wide green eyes more slowly than usual and her throat moves on a big swallow. This isn't good. I don't want her to be uncomfortable about asking for what she wants. I rest my hand on her arm. "Just say what's on your mind. Nothing you can say will be taken badly, okay?"

"I'm nervous," she admits. "Nervous that I'll ask for what I want, and I won't be able to handle it."

"You want us all, but you're worried it'll be too much?"

She nods, biting at the edge of her finger, cheeks flushing and eyes wide. My dick thickens against my underwear, already ready for whatever she has in mind.

"You don't have to worry," Dalton says. "It's your first time. We'll be careful, and anytime you want to stop, all you have to do is ask."

"Okay," she says softly, and I remove my hand so that she can finish the rest of her drink. "Let's do this before your dad gets home."

The way Gabriella says those words is filled with determination. She gulps down the rest of the vodka, slamming the glass on the counter with gusto, and all the while, my mind tries to process that this is really going to happen. I don't think I've ever been more excited about anything in my whole damned life. I don't know about my brothers, but this has been a fantasy that I've had forever. As soon as we admitted to each other that we had the same more-than-friend level feelings about Gabriella, I imagined her at the center of all of us. An angel worshiped by three mere mortals.

Kain leads the way with an inscrutable expression. Gabriella climbs the stairs behind him, her eyes drifting over photos of us as scrappy kids. Dalton and I share a look that's loaded with intensity. This shouldn't feel like such a massive step. We've already all had sex with Gabriella separately, so nothing about the act will be new. But so much feels different.

Kain heads to his room, probably because he's sure it's neat. Kain has always been the tidiest of us. In the room, Gabriella rests her bag on the floor by the door and immediately heads over to the window, staring into her own bedroom from a vantage point she probably doesn't remember. While Mom was alive, this room was her sewing and reading room, and Kain and I shared, sleeping on bunk beds.

"Our rooms are so close," she says. "You can see right into mine."

"A fact that Kain has kept to himself," Dalton says. He looks relaxed, with his hands tucked into the pockets of his worn jeans, but the tightness in his jaw tells me otherwise.

"He had fun looking into it the other day, didn't you, Kain?"

It's the first time we're being open about our exhibitionism, and Gab squeezes her legs together as Kain's heated gaze scans her, remembering.

Her eyes are drawn to me as I close the door and slide the lock into place. The scrape of metal-on-metal sounds like punctuation. The start of something that I feel we're all powerless to resist. Who's going to make the first move to get this started? I imagine it will be me, but Kain is closest, and my brother is filled with a sudden urgency that propels him two steps until he's directly in front of Gabriella. Watching him slide his big hand into the hair at her nape is enough to fully harden my cock. She stares up at him with wide eyes, half fearful, half aroused.

"Watching you come the other day was so fucking sexy," he growls.

He leans down to kiss her passionately, then scoops her

up, gripping her ass with just one hand, carrying her to the bed. I guess all the sexual tension he's been building has made him urgent and decisive.

When Gabriella is perched on the mattress, Kain kneels at her feet, untying her sneakers, encouraging her to remove her joggers. Last of all, she lifts the sweatshirt over her head, leaving just the sexist black lingerie I've ever seen. Barely there, her nipples are practically peeking over the half-cups. Between her legs, just a scrap of lace covers her pussy, leaving almost nothing to the imagination. Kain sighs as he looks her over.

Dalton sits on the edge of the mattress next to Gabriella and her eyes widen as she turns to look at him. When he bends to kiss her too, she moans low and long. A rush of heat pools behind my cock as I watch both my brothers touch and kiss her, taking turns until she's squirmy and needy.

Kain tears his T-shirt over his head in one rough movement, and I move closer, shoving my shorts down my hips and pulling off my shirt. I bounce on my feet, feeling antsy as my body fills with adrenaline.

Fuck, Gabriella looks so good between my brothers.

"Lay back," I tell her, climbing onto the bed on the opposite side to Dalton. The mattress shifts, and she leans towards me, capturing my mouth with a soft and sweet kiss before she lays back.

I ease her bra strap over her shoulder and indicate to Dalton that he should do the same. When her breasts are bare, I tease her nipple with my finger, running around and around until her skin is gooseflesh and her nipple is the tightest, most tempting peak.

While Dalton and I are busy, Kain slides Gabriella's tiny panties over her thighs and spreads her legs. Gab seems tense for a minute, but when Kain's tongue touches her clit, she sighs, staring at each of us with wide eyes as we work on giving her pleasure.

"How does she taste?" I ask, knowing full well that she's sweeter than honey.

"Like apple pie," Kain says, kissing the inside of her thigh before he returns to his dessert. Gab's hips shift, as though she needs more, but it's already too much.

"She's close already," Dalton murmurs, and it sounds like a warning. We can keep going and let her come or we can slow the pace and make her wait.

Kain doesn't seem interested in delaying her gratification. He slides a finger inside her and does something that makes her grunt her appreciation.

"So soft and warm and tight, aren't you, Angel?" he says. I want to feel too, so I do, reaching down and sliding my index finger alongside my brother's. Gabriella wriggles, pushing down so we're in as deep as we can be.

"Dalton," she gasps, pushing at his hand. He takes her request on board and, carefully, allowing her time to stretch, pushes his thick finger in too.

I press down on the inside of her thigh and Dalton does the same, opening her wide and restraining her, too. She's totally within our power, speared on our fingers, clutching tightly and moaning as Dalton uses the pad of his thumb to stroke her clit.

"Oh god," she groans. "Please."

The slick sound of her arousal fills the room as we pump our fingers, working to tip her over the edge. It's what she wants, isn't it?

"Oh…don't…stop…oh…fuck." She grinds against our fingers, and then spasms, leaking her arousal all over our hands.

And fuck if it's not the sexiest thing I've ever seen.

She gasps for air, resting her hand over her heart as she dwells behind her eyelids in the well of pleasure we dug for her.

I draw my finger from inside her and lick it clean, savoring the most beautiful woman I've ever had the pleasure of having sex with, palming my cock, which is rigid and aching.

Will Kain fuck her first? We didn't decide on how this would work, but he's gone the longest since he benefited from the deal. If it plays out that way, it'll be me last. But that doesn't seem to be what Kain has in mind.

He kneels on the mattress between her spread legs and bends to kiss her lips. "Are you okay?" he asks.

"Yes," she whispers.

"Do you want to carry on?"

A single nod confirms her answer.

"We can take you one at a time," he says, trailing a finger of her cheek, "Or we can be with you at the same time. We'll go slow if that's what you want to try."

Her eyes are fixed on his when she nods, so caught up in his words that she's barely breathing. Kain turns to me. "Lie on your back," he says, taking charge like he usually does. If he wasn't so good at it, I'd accuse him of being a bossy asshole.

I do as he instructs, lying next to Gab, who's encouraged to roll into a kneeling position and climb on top of me. Her hair trails over my skin, soft as a bird's wing, and I rest my hands on the outside of her thighs as she sits on mine. Dalton tosses me a condom and I ready my cock for what's coming next.

Kain murmurs instructions to Dalton, who removes his clothes, and climbs onto the bed next to us. Gabriella's eyes drift between my pierced cock and Dalton's unpierced dick, and her mouth drops open. Behind her, Kain deals with the condom.

Dalton strokes Gabriella's back, making her eyes roll closed. "You're so pretty, honey," he says. Part of me wants to laugh at my huge older brother's softness, but when Gab visibly relaxes, I'm grateful that he's willing to be gentle in front of us.

Kain climbs closer, gathering Gab's hair into a ponytail in his big hand. She moans as he gently tugs, letting her know he's in control. When he kisses her neck, she almost purrs, and Dalton palms her breasts, weighing each one in hands that seem giant against her frame.

Kain uses his grip to turn Gab's head, and when their eyes are locked, he tells her exactly what's going to happen.

"You're going to ease yourself onto Blake's cock, okay? And when you're good and slippery, I'm going to bend you over and push inside, too." She whimpers and her thighs clench against mine. "And when you're so stuffed full of me and Blake, you're going to take Dalton deep into your pretty throat like the good girl I know you are."

She moans when he kisses her, now completely in his thrall. Without drawing away from his kiss, she shuffles forward, taking hold of my waiting cock and notching it at her entrance. She moans again as she shifts, and I take hold of her hips and push until I'm buried deep inside her.

Damn. It feels good. So good I close my eyes and grit my teeth and count backwards from ten to force back the pleasure.

"Shit," Dalton mutters, his eyes between her legs. "Does that feel good, Angel?"

She draws back from Kain's kiss and stares down at me, letting her hands roam over my chest and the ink and muscle there. "Yeah. Blake feels good."

"I bet he does," Dalton says, pinching her little nipple until the end is pink. Her sweet little pussy ripples around my cock in response. "Fuck my brother, princess. Make him feel good."

Gabriella rests her hand flat on my chest, leaning forward so she can undulate her hips. Our eyes stay locked, and I hold on to her waist, loving the pace of her movements. After a while, Kain's hand urges her forward until she's flat against me. She pants a little, the uncertainty of what's to come making her grip my arm tightly.

Kain drops her hair, running his hands over her ribs and waist, and lower over her hips and ass. "You ready for me?" he asks. Gab nods, but the tension in her body is palpable. It's already a tight squeeze with only my cock in her pussy. I know it's possible for Kain to fit too, but it's going to take some work on his part and a whole lot of trust on hers. If she can't relax her muscles enough, this isn't going to work.

There's no pressure other than the fact that none of us want to disappoint Gabriella. We want to make this a memorable exploration of a forbidden fantasy.

You want more than just a fantasy. I don't want to admit it to myself but it's there behind every interaction, a need that feels like a hook that links me to her.

Behind all my arousal is the desire to make this so good for Gabriella that she won't ever want to be with anyone other than us. I want her to look at me, Kain, and Dalton and see men who will take care of her in every way possible.

I want her to want us for more than just this deal.

So much depends on this being explosively good for her. Sex is a physical act, but it's laced with different layers of emotion. More for women, or so I've been told.

For me, I've generally been able to separate out the physical from any emotion. I like to have fun with my sexual partners and I'm always transparent about my expectations from any encounter. This is the first time I feel deceitful.

Would Gab want to go through with this if she thought we were all pining for her to be our girlfriend? Probably not.

This whole agreement was built on the foundation of

an imminent end date. Maybe that's what Gabriella wants. Pleasure with the safety of knowing her heart doesn't have to get involved. Or, and I hope this is the case, she could want more.

I touch her cheek, needing to convey some of what I'm feeling. Baby steps.

So many words form and die on my tongue.

But now's not the time or place to express deep feelings.

Now's the time to make fantasies come true.

15

GABRIELLA

When Blake touches my cheek, it feels too gentle to be about sex. It's too tender not to be borne out of emotional feelings. I swallow down the tightness in my throat and reach for his hand, clasping it tightly in mine as Kain begins to press inside me.

This moment will remain forever in my mind. I feel fractured by the intensity of this experience. Broken and splayed open.

As I clutch at Blake, and Dalton smooths his hand over my back, my body opens to accommodate Kain. The stretching stings at first and I grit my teeth, willing myself to bear it because I don't want to fail, and I know it'll be worth it in the end. Kain crowds me, his legs pushing against the backs of my thighs, his big body looming over mine. I'm pressed between him and Blake like peanut butter and jelly between two thick wedges of bread, lost in the inky blackness behind my eyelids.

"Breathe," Blake whispers. "Breathe. This part is the most difficult. Just imagine your body opening. Imagine it giving way."

"Think about us both being deep inside you…your

pussy spread wide for us," Kain says, pressing a kiss between my shoulder blades. "Your body is ours, Gabriella." His finger brushes between the cheeks of my ass, a touch so forbidden but so arousing, all I can do is shiver.

"You're so fucking perfect," Blake murmurs again, kissing my lips gently. It's such a contrast to the intrusion between my thighs.

"You're doing so great," Dalton says, reassuring me with a sweet touch on my shoulder.

Kain strokes my hips and thighs like he's trying to calm a skittish horse and I close my eyes, relishing the caring affection they find so easy to give me. But even as I slip into a mindset of enjoying how attentive they are, the part of me that always struggles to live in a happy moment without already forecasting change worries.

I can't get attached to Blake, Dalton, and Kain. I can't let my feelings of love and familiarity forged in the past get too tangled with emotions that seem to be creeping into our sexual relationships. Maybe they're getting mixed up with what this deal is about. Maybe they're secretly hoping this will turn into something more.

But how can it?

Travis would be devastated, and I couldn't live with myself for fracturing their friendship from the inside out. Our parents would never understand. Hell, the world would never understand. I've seen the trials and tribulations Ellie's had to go through and I don't think I'm strong enough to do the same. I don't think I could ever trust anyone enough to risk the humiliation of three men breaking up with me.

I have to keep my feelings constrained to physical release. I have to focus on the way they make my body feel and isolate my heart from being touched. A loving relationship is something I want for my future, but this can't fulfill that need.

It can't.

"Kain," I whisper. "It's okay. I'm ready."

His hands pause on my waist and his cock kicks inside me. I rest up on my arms, focusing on Dalton's cock, wondering how I'm going to be able to pleasure him with my mouth. Surely my jaw won't stretch that far.

I lean closer, licking the tip, swirling my tongue around in a way that makes him hiss. Kain begins to move, in and out, in and out, stretching me open so wide it must look obscene. I wish I had his vantage point. If I got to see the explicit visual of two huge cocks in my pussy, I'd probably come immediately. I'm already close, my previous epic orgasm feeling like it happened in the distant past.

Dalton's hand rests against my neck, and he uses his fingers to support my movements. I start shallow, taking just the head of his huge dick into my mouth, giving my jaw time to open. He tastes and smells so good, and the way he moans when I manage to move a little deeper fills me with longing. I want this big man with gentle hands to feel good. I want to repay his tenderness with the most pleasure a person can experience.

Blake's hands roam over my breasts, squeezing gently and then pinching my nipples with harder intent. Like a line of electric wire, the sensation connects to my pussy, causing a fluttering that makes Kain swear.

"She likes that," he tells his brother. "She likes that a lot."

I like it so much I moan around Dalton's cock, which he really appreciates. I guess the little vibrations feel good.

Kain's thrusts have been regular and measured, a slow build to something more frenzied, and when he can't hold himself back anymore, he rests his hand on the small of my back. And fuck, when he presses against my body, my clit rubs perfectly against Blake's pubic bone every time he moves.

I stare up at Dalton and there is so much in his expression; passion, lust; disbelief and reverence. His thighs begin to shake, and I know I've got him. My jaw aches at the stretch, but I don't stop. I won't stop. Not until I taste him on my tongue and watch his reserve crumble.

"Fuck, Angel…don't stop." Dalton's voice is twisted with anticipation, his fingers flexing against my neck, and he loses control.

His cock does the impossible, and swells to even larger proportions and then he pulls back, coming into the palm of his hand.

"Hey," I say. "That was mine."

With glazed eyes, Dalton drops back onto the bed, cradling his cock like it's too sensitive for even the air to make contact with it.

"One down," Blake says, grinning up at me. He puts his hands behind his head, relaxing like he's sunning himself on the beach, leaving Kain to do all the work. It's funny how this dynamic replicates what they're like in real life.

"Slacker," I say, but I'm laughing rather than being critical. I don't need his hands when I have his cock inside me. I don't need him to move when his brother is handling that part like a pro. My clit aches to come, heat spilling like warm water from my belly to my slick pussy.

"Don't worry, Gab. I've got us all," Kain says.

"Don't worry, Gab. Super Kain to the rescue," Blake teases.

"We can switch places if you want," Kain suggests, but Blake isn't interested. He's not competitive at all.

"That's cool. You do your control-freak shit."

I bend to kiss the smile off Blake's face, and it works.

"You look so fucking sexy, Gab," Blake tells me.

"She's a goddess," Dalton adds, finally back in the land of the living.

"She's perfect," Kain says, as he thrusts deeper, and I feel like I'm going to break open from the pleasure. Blake slicks his thumb and finds my clit, and after only a few fast, tight circles, it happens.

My body convulses, flopping against Blake's warm, hard chest as Kain rests his arm on the bed next to us, pounding hard. "Oh god," I moan. "Oh god…"

"Oh, fuck." The rippling of my orgasm must trigger something in Kain and Blake, because they're only a little behind me. They release at the same time, Blake arching his back and Kain holding onto me so tightly I can barely breathe.

Dalton makes a contented humming sound and when I open my eyes, I find him turned to watch us. He pushes my damp hair back from my cheek. "Beautiful," he says.

And for some unknown reason, I feel like crying.

Why do they have to be like this? Why do they have to make me feel special?

I can't even move to put some distance between us so I can unscramble my emotions. Slowly, Kain withdraws, but he stays braced over me, kissing my neck and my back, as attentive with the aftercare as he is with the fucking.

Blake's chest is still heaving, but his fingers lace with mine.

Dalton takes my other hand, bringing it to his soft lips, his beard rough against my skin.

And I feel like I might break apart from the expanding balloon of my feelings that only get bigger with every second we spend entwined like this.

Group sex isn't supposed to be loving. I've seen enough online to know. It's supposed to be raw and a little violent. It's supposed to make the woman feel subject to the desires of the men involved. But that's not how this feels at all.

I close my eyes and try to focus on mundane things that will settle my heart, but memories of Blake, Kain, and Dalton swim into my vision. I recall a day our moms took us on a hike but didn't bring any swim clothes. When we came across a lake, we all stripped off to our underwear, the boys in their Spiderman briefs and me in my pink butterfly panties. It was weird at first, but once we were in the water, we had so much fun. After, our moms dried us off with a spare sweater, and we went home commando, our wet underwear packed in the picnic basket.

Such a silly memory but laced with so much affection.

And that's the problem. Whenever I think about these men, I struggle to unpick who they are today, and the deal we've made, with who they've been to me in the past.

They'll always be those boys who looked after me like a sister.

And I'll always be that girl who looked up to them.

Eventually, Kain rises, and I draw back from Blake, easing off his cock, which still feels hard. As I move, a strange sensation makes me look between my legs and then down at the condom. It's torn, and whatever went inside me when Blake came is now leaking out of me. He notices my sudden intake of breath and then the state of the condom, and he shoots up into a seated position.

"Shit, Gabriella. Fuck."

"What?" Dalton asks.

"The condom broke," Blake admits, peeling it away from his cock, his actions jerky and rough.

"Fuck, Blake," Kain snaps. "Didn't you realize?"

"No, douchebag. If I did, don't you think I would have said something?"

"It's okay," I say, hating to hear them speak to each other with anger. "I'm due my period in a couple of days.

I'm sure it's fine."

"It's not fine." Kain stands and paces the room. "We don't want to put you in this position. Not after what happened with Ellie."

Blake mutters something under his breath and I put my hands between my legs, trying to catch the warm fluid. Knowing Blake came inside me makes me feel hot and aroused behind the slight panic. So weird.

"Gab knows that if something like that happened, we'd be there for her, though." Dalton says it like it's a well-known fact rather than something I've never considered. They'd be there for me in what way?

Blake touches my arm tentatively, his expression solemn and guilty. "Yeah, Gabriella. Of course we'd be there for you."

"Be there to sort the problem?" I ask.

"Be there, period." The firm tone in Kain's voice takes me by surprise. Are they saying what I think they're saying? Babies are not on my immediate agenda, but definitely exist in my future plans. I was shocked when Colby, Micky, and Seb were so supportive of Ellie keeping the baby. Men in their early twenties aren't generally into child-rearing, especially when it's unplanned.

"It'll be fine," I say, even as I say a silent prayer for my period to come on schedule.

"It will be," Dalton says. "Whatever happens."

As I start to rise, ready to put my clothes back on and return home to clean myself up, there's a bang downstairs.

"I'm home," Lukas's voice bellows up the stairs.

"Fuck," Blake hisses, jumping off the bed and scrambling for his clothes.

"He won't come up here, will he?" I step off the bed and onto shaky legs. Between my legs, I feel wet and deliciously used.

"Maybe." Dalton's already half-dressed and so is Kain. "If he does, he's going to wonder why we're all in here together in the dark."

Kain quickly flips the light switch and then dashes to the window and flings it open.

My panties are damp as soon as I pull them on, but I'm dressed again in record time. "What shall I do?"

"Closet," Kain says.

Feeling ridiculous, like a kid in high school, I dash for the open door and pull it closed behind me. It's dark and smells just like Kain and I breathe him in, trying to regulate my pounding heart.

There's a knock at the door and Kain tells his dad to come in.

"What are you guys doing?" Lukas asks in his familiar, gravelly voice. If I'm not mistaken, there's a slight slur.

"Just hanging out," Blake says. "Kain's got a game coming up. He's telling us about some of Coach's new tactics."

"Okay." Lukas clears his throat. "Dalton, you should be heading to bed now. We've got a big day tomorrow."

"I will." Two sets of feet exit the room and then another. Blake must have decided it would be more natural for him to leave, too.

I wait for what feels like a lifetime before Kain opens the door. "The coast is clear," he whispers. "Dad's gone to bed."

"That was so close," I say. "A few minutes earlier, and he would have heard some noises that none of us would be able to explain."

"Exactly."

I step out into the brightness of Kain's room, smoothing my hair and flexing my shoulders. My body feels wrecked and so does my heart. "I should go," I say. I need to walk around the corner to get my car.

"I'll walk you," Kain says.

"Won't your dad wonder what you're doing?"

"He's already snoring," Kain laughs. "You'll hear it when we're in the hallway."

I pick up my purse and watch as Kain looks left and right, checking the coast is clear. "Now," he whispers, and I follow him down the stairs and out into the cool night air.

There's a stillness about this time of night when most people are inside watching TV or sleeping. Even the birds are silent. Only the rustling trees interrupt the quiet as we tread a careful path to the sidewalk. "Blake's mortified about what happened," Kain says, as we reach my car.

"He doesn't have to be," I say. "It's not on him. We were all there."

"Yeah, but that stupid fucking piercing."

I shake my head. "It might not have been that. The friction between the two of you could have caused the tear."

Kain nods. "Just…" He puts his hands in his pockets, widening his stance. In the darkness, his hair and beard are almost black, his sapphire eyes like portals to another world. "...you have to know that we'd never leave you to deal with anything on your own. I know we said this is a no-strings deal, and it wouldn't be ideal for Travis to find out, but we'd deal with that, okay? We'd take care of you."

I inhale an involuntarily shaky breath, feeling the burn of tears in my throat. The words 'no-strings' sting even though they shouldn't. I agreed to this. I wanted this. But somehow, hearing the words now from Kain's lips hurts.

"Nothing's going to happen," I say confidently, masking my wobbly feeling. "Thanks for walking me back."

"Of course," he says.

"I guess I'll see you."

He nods and takes a step closer. With two hands, he cradles my face and I let my eyes drift closed before he kisses me. It's sweet and affectionate and loaded with more feeling than any no-string arrangement should contain.

I pull away more quickly than I intend and feel regret as soon as I see Kain's expression fall.

"Tell Blake everything's fine, okay?" I say, finding my keys in my purse and opening the car.

"I will."

I force a smile as I close the car door, then throw it into drive. I reach home before Kain, and I don't wait for him. In my house, I lean against the front door and shake my head.

Maybe a few days' space will bring things back to where they need to be. A few days' space and the arrival of my period.

16

DALTON

Gabriella's coming over for dinner tonight. Kain and Blake have agreed to take Dad out and keep him away long enough for us to enjoy an evening together.

It wasn't easy to convince them, but they both owe me, and I called in those favors.

Romantic meals for two weren't supposed to be part of our deal, but over the last three weeks, Gabriella has taken time to teach me to cook every meal I've bought ingredients for, and tonight, I want to say thank you.

I want her to understand what a difference it's made to me to know I'm capable of doing more than construction. It's a path I've always seen laid out before me, my father's dream, but it's never made me feel alive. I didn't really know what that would feel like until recently.

The house is tidy. The food is ready. I glance at myself in the mirror, smoothing my beard and adjusting my hair. I've bought a new shirt for tonight and teamed it with my best dark blue jeans. It's important to me that Gabriella feels that I've made an effort for her.

When the bell rings, I stride toward the door, knowing

she's probably worried about getting spotted on our doorstep.

"Hey," I say, finding Gabriella looking gorgeous in a green shirt dress and bright white sneakers. Her eyes move down the length of me, and she moistens the middle of her bottom lip, already thinking about sex. It's only taken me a month to be able to pick up her sexual tells. In fact, I think she might be the horniest girl I've ever met.

"Hey, Dalton."

When I close the door, she steps close, wrapping her arms around my neck and pulling me in for a kiss. In seconds, she deepens the kiss, moaning against my lips, her tongue tangling with mine. Instantly, my body is primed, but I'm wary. She's been this way since the night Blake's condom split; totally focused on sex. Different from the first time we were together when she snuggled up against me and seemed to relish my affection.

She got her period the next day, so there weren't any repercussions to our group experience, but ever since, she's been fixated on getting to the physical act as quickly as possible, asking for us to be cold and domineering, resisting and avoiding any kind of aftercare.

Tonight, I don't want to just fuck her. I want to spend time with her like we used to and hear about what's been going on in her life. I want to feed her and show her how good I am at doing something that was totally outside of my skill set until she came along.

It takes all my powers of resistance to put my hands on her shoulders and ease her back. "You ready for dinner?"

"I'm hungry for you," she says, reaching down to cup my dick.

"And I'm hungry for you, too, but first, I want us to eat. The food is ready." I know I don't imagine the flash of panic in her eyes, but I plow on, hoping that she'll relax once she sees what I've prepared. "It's your favorite," I say. "Irish stew with mashed potatoes."

"You made stew?" Her eyebrows form a disbelieving arch that makes me chuckle.

"Better." I smile. "I made *your* stew."

I take her hand and lead her to the kitchen. I haven't set the table with anything fancy. I wanted to but thought if she saw a rose in a vase, or fancy napkins, she might run for the hills.

She inhales as she sits at the chair that I hold out for her. "It smells good, Dalton. Almost as good as mine." The last part is said with a mischievous grin and I'm immediately relieved to see her relaxing a little.

"Wait until you taste it."

It's stupid that I feel nervous about serving her. It's just a meal. Just meat and potatoes, after all. Except, it's so much more. It's like I'm baring my soul. A soul I didn't know I had until Gabriella gently inspired me.

I try to assemble her plate like a picture I saw online. It doesn't come out exactly as I hoped. It smells so good, though, that I hope she'll forgive the rustic presentation.

"Here," I say, setting her heaped plate down in front of her. Gabriella breathes in the steam and nods her head. I don't serve myself until she takes a bite and I watch her react to the flavors; my heart lodges in my throat until she smiles.

"Wow…that is delicious, Dalton. Are you sure you didn't buy it from a restaurant?"

I rest my hand on my heart and pretend to be offended. "You wound me."

"Seriously." She heaps another mouthful and chews. Her eyes are wide and appreciative, and I find myself holding my breath. "So good."

It's only when she's confirmed it's good that I heap my plate with the food, and when I sit across from her to eat,

I'm salivating.

My first mouthful of tender meat in a rich sauce and creamy potatoes is like heaven. I'm so proud of myself that my chest expands like a peacock. Like, seriously, I never thought I could make something so good.

Gabriella pours herself some red wine and takes a sip before she dabs her lips. "Did you practice?" she asks.

I shake my head. "I just wrote everything down when I got home," I say. "I've started compiling a recipe book of the things you've taught me."

"Don't go trying to sell it," she jokes. "Those recipes are trademarked by the Cross family."

"I would never," I say seriously.

"Although…" Gab pauses, glancing up to the left. "Have you ever thought about going to culinary school?"

"What? No!"

"Don't dismiss the idea like that. I'm serious."

I rest my fork-holding hand on the table, scanning her face to gauge the genuineness of her comments and find her expression earnest. "You think I could?" I ask.

"I think you really have potential."

"My dad wouldn't like it," I say, cringing at how immature I sound and my instinct to try to keep him happy.

"Your dad doesn't have to like it," she reminds me carefully.

I bite my bottom lip as the idea settles. Construction has been my destiny for as long as I can remember. Dad always talked about us going into the family business, and as a dutiful eldest son, I just did what he expected, especially after Mom died. I didn't want to be a burden to him or cause him disappointment in any way. But although I get a lot out of physical exertion, the building industry doesn't light my fire.

It's profitable. At the end of the day, it gives us a good life. There's never been a time when we've been short of money. My dad isn't an educated man, but he's a skilled builder and he understands people. All our clients love us. We never advertise because we get so much recommended business that we can never take it all on.

Could I do something else?

What would it feel like to wake up in the morning and not put on my work trousers and steel-toed boots? I've gotten so accustomed to this way of life; I can't even comprehend what doing something else would look like.

I tell Gabriella that and she reaches out to touch my arm. "I know you love your dad, and you want to make him happy. That's admirable, Dalton. That shows respect and empathy. It shows that you're grateful for his sacrifices. Maybe, if he had a choice to do something else, he would have ended up in a totally different career. Have you ever thought of that?"

"I guess that makes it worse. He didn't have a choice."

"So now you have to reject the fact that you do?"

I lean back in my chair and press my lips between my teeth.

Gabriella eats another mouthful and rolls her eyes with pleasure, underlining her argument. "You know, I've made this stew so many times with my mom and without her, but somehow yours tastes better."

"I added a little more ale and a teaspoon of brown sugar to give it more richness," I admit.

"Really? Where did those ideas come from?" She points her fork at me like she wants to accentuate the point she is making.

"I just made it up."

"Because you have a talent. An instinct."

I settle back into eating, using the time it takes to chew

to absorb Gabriella's suggestion more fully. Could I do it?

And then I realize that's not the question I should be asking. *Do I want to do it* is the right question.

When we're done with the food, I take Gabriella up to my room, where she immediately tries to climb me like a tree, but I need time to digest. Instead of fucking her, I tuck her into my bed and put on a comedy special, wanting us to watch something lighthearted together. I want to hear her laugh and build a connection outside of just sex.

She initially seems wary, but eventually snuggles into my chest.

The show is hilarious, and it feels so good to relax in Gabriella's company. The deal wasn't supposed to encompass any of what we've done tonight, but I don't feel bad for pushing the boundaries of our arrangement. What I want from Gabriella is way more complex than just a fuck buddy relationship.

I know that I shouldn't add complexity to this situation. Travis's face pops into my head as her hand works its way beneath my shirt and caresses the ridges of muscle on my belly.

But everything we're doing is wrong. Adding a little date-night sauce onto a sex ice cream doesn't seem capable of making the current situation much worse.

And the fact that Gabriella isn't running out the door tells me she's okay with it, too.

When the comedian takes his bow, I flip her onto her tummy and give her what she wants, holding her down while I take her apart piece by piece and then put her back together again.

17

GABRIELLA

"The music is electric tonight," Celine yells, her right arm pumping the air like she's pulling a whistle on an old steam locomotive.

"Yeah. Apparently, the DJ's a freshman with some awesome skills." I yell back, dancing and trying to focus on enjoying the moment. The Red Devil has always been my favorite bar, and we always have a great time here, but tonight I feel under pressure to be bubbly, as though I'm putting on a front. I can't resist the urge to scan the far corners, hunting for three specific men. The pull they have on me makes me feel weak, an emotion I'm wholly uncomfortable with.

Over Celine's shoulder, I spy some movement by the bar. Ellie has arrived, with Colby, Sebastian, and Micky. Behind them, Dornan, and some of the football team lumber in, blocking the entryway until one of the doormen barks at them to move inside.

I glance at my watch, wondering where Kain, Dalton, and Blake are. Maybe they've thought twice about coming to celebrate my birthday. When I invited them, they seemed pleased, but when I told them we'd have to pretend that there's nothing going on between us, their faces fell.

I was annoyed at first because this deal was always supposed to be a secret, and they made me feel like the bad guy for not wanting to kiss them all in public. I don't know what they expected, but we're not in that place. We can never be in that place. Gossip spreads like wildfire. There's no containing it.

And if Travis found out…

I shake my head even at the idea of him rushing back from Germany to confront us.

"Why is your face like that?" Celine asks. She tosses her auburn curls over her shoulder and wrinkles her freckled button nose. "It's your birthday. You're supposed to be happy.

"I am happy," I say.

She frowns and purses her lips. "Something's going on with you, and I don't know what it is."

I've kept details of the deal to myself. Even Ellie, who encouraged me to go for it, doesn't know what we've been doing. It's easier to keep it a secret rather than face up to the obvious questions that any of my friends would ask.

Celine turns to the bar and waves as Ellie starts to make her way to us, her dancing walk through the bobbing throngs of people making me smile despite all my angst.

"I am so happy to be out tonight; you guys don't even understand."

Hugging Ellie tightly, it hits me how different her life is now. "Who's looking after Noah tonight?"

"My mom. Any excuse to have cuddles. I swear, she's so great at being a nana. I didn't expect it at all."

"That's good to hear," I say. My friend didn't plan to become a mom so young, and knowing she's got family support is a relief. She's never been good at asking for help. Like me, she doesn't trust easily. Maybe that's what drew us together, a familiar wariness.

"Have you guys been drinking? Colby's buying me a Red Devil. I'm practically salivating. Can you believe it's been a year and a half since I drank one?"

"Seriously?"

"Yeah. With the pregnancy and breastfeeding…I just haven't been able to."

"I'm still over here dealing with bullshit like which ramen I should buy at the store and you're raising a whole human," Celine says.

"I don't have to worry about ramen," Ellie says. "I leave Colby to do all the grocery shopping."

"Lucky you," I say, glancing at the huge man responsible for feeding my friend. His arms are bulging against his shirtsleeves, probably from all the groceries he's been hefting!

The dance floor becomes more crowded as Colby, Micky, and Seb shoulder their way through, each holding a red cocktail and a bottle of beer.

"Happy birthday, Gabs," Seb says, planting a kiss on my cheek. He hands me a Red Devil. Micky passes one to Celine and Colby gives his to Ellie. We clink our glasses, and they both yell happy birthday before we drink them down in big, freezing gulps.

"Wow," I gasp. "That was good."

"Look who it is," Colby yells, nodding at someone in the doorway. I peek around his bulky shoulder to find Kain nodding and smiling back. Behind him, Dalton and Blake are searching the crowd for us. I put up my hand to wave but pull it down quickly, embarrassed. I've forgotten how to be natural. Would I wave at them, and smile if I wasn't having sex with them? Ugh. I hate that sex makes everything complicated.

"Oooo…Kain is looking fine," Ellie says, licking the

cocktail from her lips, eyes gleaming with suggestiveness. "And are they his brothers?"

"Yeah," I say. "Dalton's the big one, and Blake's the one with the tats."

"Yowzer. That's a trifecta of hotness right there."

Seb throws his arm around Ellie's shoulder. "You know we're standing right here?"

She kisses his cheek. "Of course I know. Why? Are you jealous?"

As they continue their jokey conversation, my focus zeroes in on Kain's tall frame. At six-two, he stands a few inches taller than a lot of the men in here, but amongst the football crowd, he just seems normal sized. I watch as Kain shakes hands with Dornan and a few of the other players on his team. Some know his brothers. Others get introductions. Dalton seems restless, as though he doesn't want to be dragged into game talk. He whispers something in Kain's ear, and he and Blake draw away, heading straight for me.

Shit.

This is weird.

I can do anything with these men. Hell, I've sucked their dicks and sat on their faces. I've been fucked in just about every position I'm flexible enough to achieve. But somehow, greeting them in a social setting seems weirdly intimate. They've seen me naked so why does dancing in front of them make me cringe.

"Happy birthday, Gabriella," Dalton says when he reaches our group. His big hand cradles my elbow as he leans in to give me a chaste kiss on the cheek. It's just right for the kind of relationship we're supposed to have, and I'm grateful that he's listened to my rules for tonight, but my heart presses against my chest wall uncomfortably. My hands itch to touch him, my arms ache to embrace him. When he steps to the side so Blake can greet me, too, the space between us feels cold and sad. When my eyes meet Blake's, a sizzle of electricity passes between us and I have to lower my lids momentarily to regroup. His kiss on my cheek is equally chaste, but his hand on my waist is not and I shiver from the buzz of nerves that climb my spine and scalp.

Fuck.

I'm a mess. A mess of a human being who doesn't know what she wants. There's no way I'm going to be able to stand near them and not react. They're like magnets, drawing me into their orbit, sending all my senses scrambling.

"So, are you going to introduce me?" Celine asks, her eyes scanning the length of Dalton lasciviously. He's definitely her type. She likes her men big and brawny. Her current boyfriend, Eddie, is a little like Dalton in appearance although they're nothing alike in personality.

"This is Dalton, and this is Blake. They're Kain's brothers."

"Kain's brothers! Hi, I'm Celine."

They smile at her politely but seem uncomfortable with the flirty way she's looking at them. There's a pause that I don't know how to fill. My tongue is tied and my mouth is dry.

A hand rests on my shoulder from behind. A hand joined to a man who smells just like Kain. When I turn, he smiles down at me, and winks a piercing blue eye. "Hey, birthday girl."

"Hey yourself." I turn and give him a kiss on the cheek, hoping I can avoid any flutterier feelings if I just take control and keep things businesslike. I check to see if Celine is watching, but she's dancing with Ellie.

"Are you having a good time?" Kain asks.

"Yeah," I say. "Awesome." I chew my cheek, feeling the hot creep of embarrassment heat my neck.

"Hey, Gab," Ellie calls. "Come dance with us."

I join them, grateful to be saved from stilted conversation so I can lose myself with my friends.

When I get close, Ellie grabs my arm and leans in to speak into my ear. "If you're not fucking those men, I'll eat my shoe." Her eyes search mine, but I blink and look away.

"What?" I splutter and pretend to look around for who she's referring to.

"You know what I'm talking about, Gabriella Cross. Don't pretend with us. We're your besties. If you can't be honest with us about your sexual exploits, who can you be honest with?"

I sigh, knowing that there's no way I'm going to keep up any kind of denial now Ellie's got this bone between her teeth. "Okay. I'm banging them, but it's a secret. You absolutely cannot tell a soul, okay? Promise."

Celine stares at me like she's about to choke on her own tongue. Ellie throws her head back and laughs, the pretty gold chain at her throat bouncing with every chuckle. "I knew it," she says. "I absolutely knew you wouldn't be able to resist gathering your own harem."

"Shit." Celine squeezes my arm as though she's about to tell me something serious. "Now I'm the only one without a harem."

I roll my eyes, still trying to dance and maintain the appearance that I'm having a great time. "I don't have a harem. I just have three fuck buddies who need to remain a secret. It's never going to become anything serious."

"What do you mean?" Ellie asks. "Why the hell not? Are they bad in bed?"

"Hell no!" I gasp; the very idea that Kain, Dalton, and Blake can be seen as anything less than sex gods is too outrageous.

"So, what then?" She pats her curly hair and adjusts her

black mini dress. Even after having a baby, she still has a gorgeous figure. She's probably got her body back from all the amazing sex she's been having.

"They're my brother's best friends," I say, expecting my statement to draw a line underneath the conversation, but it doesn't.

"So what? That must be one of the top ten ways girls meet their significant others. I mean, what the hell's the point of having a stinky older brother if he's not going to hook you up with his hot friends?" Celine shrugs her shoulders and then glances behind me to where the Nowak brothers are chatting to Ellie's men. They're all in the middle of the dance floor but they don't seem to care.

"Do you think Eddie will be up for adding a couple more dudes to your relationship?" I joke with Celine.

"Errr…no. Definitely not. Shame though." She purses her lips, "'cos there are some hot guys in here tonight."

"Trouble in paradise?" I ask, desperate to move the focus of the conversation.

"I don't think so," she says, "although he has been a little withdrawn lately."

"That must be a relief," I say, knowing how demanding Celine's boyfriend can be. The guy has a permanent hard-on, and she's always trying to escape his voracious sexual appetite.

"I guess. I told him to come tonight, but he has something else on."

I shrug, not bothered that Eddie didn't see my birthday celebration as a priority. He's not my favorite person in the world. Celine could do so much better. I scan the crowd, wondering who she might consider hot. Dornan is looking sharp in a crisp white shirt and dark navy jeans. Elias too. Jermaine has a bandage on his face — probably an injury he picked up on the field — so he isn't looking his best. Gareth and Bobby wouldn't be her type. I guess she could be talking about a stranger.

Kain touches my arm to attract my attention. "Hey…would you like another drink?"

"You don't have to do that."

"It's your birthday," he says. "Of course I have to buy your drinks and…" he trails off, checking to see if anyone else is around, "...we each have a gift for you."

Shit. My heart makes a funny squeezing beat and I bite my bottom lip, not sure how to respond. Birthday gifts weren't a part of this deal and they definitely aren't appropriate if we're keeping our thing secret.

"Errr…thanks…"

His hand slides into his pocket, and he pulls out a tiny black box. It looks like a fucking engagement ring. "Open your purse," he whispers.

I unzip my little black pouch purse that is hanging across my body. He slides the box inside, trying to do it as quickly as possible. "You can open it later."

"I will."

Blake steps forward and bends, trying to get me to hear him clearly over the loud music. "My present is your very own Nowak original tattoo…anywhere on your body, any design."

"Really?" I gasp.

"You could even get the sleeping angel if that's what you want."

My instinct is to throw my arms around his neck, but we're surrounded by people we know. "Thanks," I mouth, holding myself tightly. "That's awesome."

Blake steps to the side, and Dalton takes his place. "My gift is at your place," he says. "You'll find it later; behind that giant pot your mom has in the front yard."

I imagine Dalton skulking around at the front of my house, searching for somewhere to hide a gift. What kind of gift would he choose to leave there rather than bring here? A big gift, potentially. "Okay," I say. "Thanks."

He forces his hands deep into the pockets of his black jeans and it feels as though he's trying to restrain himself from reaching out to me. I feel that way too. Desperate to touch them and having to use all my strength and reserve to hold me back.

Everything about this situation sucks.

More people gather on the dance floor until our corner is filled with friends here to celebrate my special day. Usually, I'd love to be the center of attention, but it feels weird, almost as though I'm playing a part and none of the feelings are mine. I dance but I am conscious of every movement, wooden where I'd usually be fluid, conscious where I would usually be filled with abandon. Celine buys more drinks and I down a shot of vodka and another Red Devil, hoping the liquid courage will make me less awkward, but it doesn't seem to work. Instead, a dark blanket settles over my heart.

My skin is magnetized to the three men who are politely socializing with my friends but should be touching me. They should be kissing me. They should be making it clear that I'm theirs and they're mine.

Except that isn't true.

We have a deal. A stupid deal that has confused me to my very core.

I'm about to make my excuse so I can head to the restroom and gather my thoughts when Celine makes a gasping sound. She's staring at her phone, with her hand pressed over her mouth. I'm quick to get closer, sensing there's something wrong. "Celine. What is it?"

She turns her phone screen in my direction, and I squint to focus on an image of what looks like a party. In the background of the picture is a man with a girl straddling his lap. I lean in, trying to make out what I'm looking at, and then I realize.

It's Eddie. Celine's boyfriend is somewhere else, with another girl in his arms.

"Oh shit," I say, grabbing the phone and holding it closer to my face, wanting to make one-hundred-percent sure before I say another word. "That asshole."

Tears begin to stream down Celine's face, and I immediately wrap my arms around her, rubbing her back and making soft, soothing noises. At first, she sags against me, her sobs wracking her body. Ellie wraps her arms around both of us, asking what's wrong in a frantic tone. "She just got a photo of Eddie cheating," I say.

"That asshole…" Ellie gasps and Celine begins to laugh in a manic way that is more worrying than the crying, pulling away and resting her hands on her knees.

"Exactly. That asshole. I mean, who the fuck does he think is? He's been hounding me about staying together. I kept telling him these are our college years, and we should be having experiences, sewing our oats. I kept trying to break up, at least to have a bit of space to breathe, and he kept saying no. And all the time, he just wanted to have his cake and eat it too. Well, fuck him. It's over. I need another drink."

Before I have an opportunity to dissuade her, Celine is striding from the dance floor to the bar. She orders an obscene number of cocktails, and Ellie and I watch with dread as she downs them all, one by one. She's okay at first, dancing like it's the last night of Cancun spring break, but then suddenly she hits a wall. All the color drains from her face and she clutches her stomach.

"We need to get her outside," I say. "Fresh air." I put my arm around Celine's waist and quickly guide her to the door. The doormen shoot me knowing looks as I bustle past them with Ellie trailing. As soon as we're in the parking lot, Celine loses the contents of her stomach, groaning loudly. I just about manage to keep her upright while she's vomiting, but then her knees go out from under her and I'm just not strong enough to manage.

"Shit," Ellie says, trying to help, but even with the two of us trying, Celine's a deadweight. She lolls forward, her eyes dropping shut, and I start to panic.

"I think she has alcohol poisoning," I say, trying to at least keep her upper body upright.

"Should we call an ambulance?"

"I don't know." The racing beat of my heart blurs my thoughts. Celine groans and my guts clench, recalling the freshman who died last year from drinking too much.

"I'll get Colby. He'll know what to do."

Ellie rushes back inside, leaving me balancing the deadweight of Celine. The poor thing is totally out of it, making more low groaning noises. She doesn't respond when I ask her if she's okay. She's dazed and confused, lost in a world of her own.

The cold creeps over my skin, my body aching from the position I'm in. But in less than two minutes, Ellie is back with a whole entourage of worried people. Colby is already on the phone calling an ambulance. Micky kneels to check Celine's pulse.

"Her heart's racing," he says, as worry furrows his brow and narrows his lips.

"Shit. Should we get her some water?" I ask.

"She'll probably just throw it up. Better wait for the ambulance. They might give her an IV."

"Right."

Micky rises to speak with Colby and Dornan squats down to check on Celine. "What the hell have you done to yourself?" he asks her softly.

"Eddie's such a stupid asshole," I say. "He's always been so fucking controlling. I just can't believe he'd be that way and cheat on her."

"I know." Dornan pushes Celine's hair back from her face so tenderly, my brow rises in surprise. "She already knew she'd be better off without him, but just didn't have the heart to let him go when he was fighting so hard to keep her."

"It's for the best," I say. "I don't know who sent that picture, but whoever it was did her a huge favor."

"I'm going to get her up," Dornan says. "Her knees must hurt on the asphalt."

In a move that takes Herculean strength, he scoops Celine up into his arms and stands. When Celine's head lolls, I rest my hand behind it, balancing her against Dornan's bulky chest. In the darkness, he looks like a Viking carrying his slain bride.

I glance around to find Elias talking with Kain, Dalton, and Blake. Dalton nods in my direction as if to say, 'we're here if you need us.' It's the sweetest gesture that hurts so bad.

Ellie strokes Celine's cheek, whispering soft reassurance, and we wait for the ambulance.

It only takes ten minutes to arrive. The paramedics take one look at Celine and decide that she needs to go to the hospital. Dornan carries her into the ambulance, resting her gently onto the gurney. I watch as he smooths her hair back from her face and bends to kiss her forehead. Again, I'm startled by his tenderness. I mean, I know we're all friends, but I don't think I've ever seen Dornan act this way before.

When he lumbers out of the ambulance, he turns to me. "Who's going to go with her?"

"I'll go," Ellie says. "It's your birthday."

"Forget it," I tell her. "You need to get home to Noah. I don't have anywhere I need to be."

I climb into the ambulance, taking a seat at Celine's feet, watching the paramedic check her blood pressure and attach an IV. When I turn, I find Dalton, Blake, and Kain looking on worriedly. I can almost feel their concern and frustration rolling from them in waves.

If our relationship was in the open, there's no way they'd be standing back this way. They must be itching to provide me with support because that's who they are. They've been raised to be good men, reliable men, strong men. All the qualities that are on my list of traits for a future partner.

As the doors are closing, I raise my hand in a small wave.

It's not the way I thought I'd be spending my birthday, but as long as Celine recovers, that'll be the best birthday gift I could receive.

In the hospital, when the doctors confirm that Celine is going to be fine, I remember Kain's gift. When I open the plush little box, I find a silver chain and a dainty angel's wing pendant. It's so pretty, and I almost tear up at the image of him searching for such a sweet gift for me.

Later, when Celine is safely home and the birds are starting to sing their dawn chorus, I finally make it home. Remembering Dalton's instructions, I find a wrapped box exactly where he described it would be. Mom's still sleeping, so I creep to the kitchen to open it.

Inside is a small chocolate cupcake covered in pink hearts. The card reads, Forgive my first attempt at baking. Happy Birthday sweet girl."

I hold the card against my heart, swallowing down the wave of emotions tonight has taken me on. I gently remove the cake from the box, pull down the wrapper, and take a huge bite. It's melt-in-the-mouth-perfect, filled with chocolatey goodness. Dalton's so damned talented, it makes me want to cry.

When I flop into bed, I struggle to sleep for a long time, now more conflicted than I have ever been.

18

BLAKE

When I finish up my current client and head to the register so that they can pay for the eagle tattoo I just spent two hours inking into their skin, I glance at my watch.

Gabriella should be here any minute.

I'm as nervous as I am excited.

This morning, Kain made me promise that I'd do my best work. "No pissing around," he said. "No jokes. Take it seriously."

Of course I intend to take it seriously. Inking something permanent onto Gabriella's perfect virgin skin is a huge responsibility, one I am not approaching lightly.

I haven't seen her since the night of her birthday last week. We've all been waiting for a message on our group WhatsApp, but nothing came through. Her absence has left us all on edge, uncertain for the reason, and facing the possible disappointment that she might be backing out of the deal. Dalton suggested that the gifts were a step too far into boyfriend territory, and I was close to agreeing when she called to arrange for me to do the tattoo. Kain has been walking around like a bear with a sore head. Dalton's shoulders have been more rounded than usual. And I've been more restless than ever. Last night, Dad jokingly threatened to toss me out the window if I didn't stop my leg from jittering. I didn't even realize it was moving.

But she did call me to arrange this tattoo and I'm hoping it's a good sign. At least it's a sign our deal hasn't run its course.

When the bell over the door rings, I glance up to find Gabriella, framed by the doorway, her golden hair tumbling over her shoulders, radiant in cut-off shorts and a pink tank.

Someone behind me makes a low whistle and I whip around to shoot Ryan a savage look. The guy is permanently horny and can get too flirty with the customers. Over my dead body he is going to flirt with my girl. Except, I can't tell him Gabriella's off-limits because I promised to keep our deal a secret.

She's not my girl. She's just a girl who uses me for sex.

The reality of that statement is a lot less satisfying than it sounds. Not that the sex isn't perfect because it absolutely is. I just want more of the package than Gabriella seems willing to give.

"Hey, Blake," she says brightly.

"Hey." My whole body screams at me to kiss her, hold her, touch her, anything! Instead, I drop my clenched fists behind the protection of the register and smile like I'm not at war with my very soul. "Ready to get your first tattoo?"

Ryan, not taking the hint, lumbers up beside me. "She's a virgin?" he asks, with a definite flirty undertone. Gabriella smiles, but I see the wariness cloud her eyes. She doesn't like him making sex jokes.

"It's her first tattoo." I try to keep my tone patient, but Gab's mouth twitches at the corner at my obvious annoyance.

I don't want to have an argument with Ryan today, but

I will if he carries on being an idiot. "This place is cool," she says, focusing on the huge graffiti mural of brightly colored tattoo imagery, the hot pink sofa, and distressed industrial wood floors. The franchise owner, Carl, has an eye for design that he carries through all Ink Factor tattoo shops. He takes a special interest in our shop because it's the nearest to the original.

"So, are you ready to work with me on the design?"

"I want what you described," she says, softly blushing at the memory.

"The sleeping angel?"

"Yes."

"Okay." I hold my hand out to guide her in the direction of my section. "This way."

As she walks in front of me, I hear Ryan whistle again and it takes all my strength not to deck him for even thinking about it. I watch Gabriella's hips sway before catching up so I can show her where to go. She takes a seat on the chair and I grab the materials I need to start the drawing. I have the tattoo clearly in my mind, so I don't look for inspiration.

"First, you need to sign the consent form. Then I'll need to take measurements for where it's going to go," I say. "Do you want it in the place we discussed?"

"Yes," she says.

Our eyes meet and the connection between us is a white-hot pulse of energy I feel in my dick. "You'll need to take off your shorts and lie back."

Gabriella doesn't read the form, trusting that it's okay for her to sign it. Then she begins to unbutton her shorts. It's odd how weirdly intimate this feels when I've seen this girl naked multiple times, but watching her wriggle out of the snug denim is such a turn on I can hardly breathe. She slides off her sandals too and when she lies back on the reclined chair, I inhale a deep breath and hold it, trying to calm the pulse of arousal that builds with every beat of my heart.

Her panties are sweet white cotton with a little pink bow in the middle, something so innocent looking that it feels obscene.

"Can you pull this side up a little?" I ask, and she gradually eases the fabric higher so that her hip is exposed. Her hip and the seam between her gorgeous thigh and other places I can't stop thinking about.

Shit. This is so damned unprofessional.

I take my paper and lay it over her warm skin, drawing a light ring around the area I have to work with. I try to concentrate on the mechanics of my profession, but it's so hard when her sweet perfume lingers in the air around us, and I'm so close to places I really want to taste.

I whip the paper away as soon as I'm done, and turn my back, taking a seat on my rolling stool. All my focus goes into trying to create the most beautiful angel I've ever drawn. I channel how I feel about Gabriella into the soft downiness of the folded wings that form a blanket around the dainty-framed celestial being. Her nose is just like Gabriella's, and her lips too. Her hair frames her face the same way Gabriella's does when she lies next to me in bed. Her hands tuck under her chin in a way that seems almost childlike, and the gauzy cloth of her dress wraps around her slender legs like ribbons.

It's so pretty. My heart swells with pride. Gabriella remains silent the whole way through, and I feel her eyes resting on my back, waiting.

"What do you think?" I ask, holding it out to her, silently praying she's going to love it.

She gasps softly, her hand flying to cover her sweet lips. "It's beautiful, Blake. So beautiful." She glances up, then down again, biting on her lip. "You've made it look a little like me."

I nod, holding her gaze with an intensity that shifts something inside me. Can she feel how I feel? Does she know how much I want her? I curse the way my mind keeps dragging me to places there is no point in visiting. "Does it?"

She smiles like she believes I'm pretending not to be aware. "Yes, Blake. It does."

"Well, you are an angel, Gab," I say. "Are you ready for me to transfer this to your skin?"

"As ready as I'll ever be," she says.

She lays back, pulling her panties back again, but that's not going to work. "Gab, I think you'll need to take those off."

"Off?" I nod, trying not to smile as she flushes a pretty shade of candy floss. "You want me to sit here with no panties on?" She eyes the door, obviously concerned that Ryan or one of the other tattooists could walk in at any second.

"I'll give you something to cover up with," I say. "Although, I think I'd prefer it if I didn't have to."

"Very funny," she scoffs, but her amusement peeks through. "Now, if we were at home, maybe. But here, you're crazy!"

I grab a strip of blue tissue and hand it to her. The way she shimmies out of her cute underwear gives me an immediate boner; one I don't fight against. She balls up the fragment of cotton and stuffs it behind herself, covering up so quickly I only get a second of the best view in the world. Her eyes drift to my crotch and when she notices the effect she's had on me, her eyebrows shoot up.

"Woh, Blake. Down, boy."

"What?" Holding my hands up, I take a step closer and lean in to whisper. "You think there's a world where you can take your panties off and show me a glimpse of your sweet little pussy and I'm not going to get hard? If there is,

I don't want to live in it."

Gabriella chews her lip, trying not to smile. "You, Blake Nowak, are terrible."

"So terrible that you love it."

"The best kind of terrible," she admits.

"Do you want numbing cream, or are you going hardcore?"

"Numbing cream all the way."

I'm relieved she's not trying to be brave. As a first timer, the incessant press of the needle into skin would be tough to take. Plus, now I get to smooth cream over Gabriella's skin, which is way more fun than watching her suffer at my hand.

I take the time to get my equipment ready and she tells me what happened at the hospital with Celine, and all the grim details of Celine's confrontation with her philandering boyfriend. When I'm sure her skin is ready, I clean away the cream and shave away any tiny downy hairs and clean the area with antibacterial soap. Gabriella watches everything. I smear petroleum jelly onto her skin and take the stencil, ready to make the transfer. I hold it above the area. "This is where I think it should go," I say. "What do you think?"

"That looks good," she says. "It's hard to see from this angle."

"I can hold a mirror?"

"Yeah. That would be good."

I take a small mirror and angle it until she says she can see the image. "Just a little higher, I think." Making the adjustment, I meet her eyes to check if it's correct. She shoots me a quick, nervous smile. "Perfect."

It doesn't take long to transfer the stencil to her skin. When I lift the paper, we both look down at the temporary image. "This is going to look so good."

She nods, this time smiling less tightly. "I hope so."

I smear more petroleum jelly over her skin and fill the ink caps. When I open a new, sterilized needle, Gabriella inhales quickly. I rest my hand on her slender leg, something I definitely wouldn't do to a client I wasn't intimate with. "It's going to be fine. I promise. Just try to relax."

"Maybe I won't look," she says.

"Yeah, that might be a good idea."

She takes a deep breath and closes her eyes. I get the machine ready and switch it on. The whirring sound startles Gab, and she laughs tightly.

"Ready?"

"As I'll ever be," she whispers.

The first press of the machine against her skin sets my heart racing. The responsibility to make this good is heavy, but I know I can do something special. I just hope she's going to love it.

I lose myself in the process, and Gabriella is so silent it's almost as though she isn't here. Only when I'm done, and I wipe it over one more time does she open her eyes.

"Don't look yet," I say. "I want you to see it in the mirror."

At the foot of the reclined chair is a full-length mirror. I help Gab to her feet, and sweetly, she keeps her eyes closed, trusting me to lead her forward. She keeps the blue paper over her pussy, but I get a perfect view of her peachy ass as she walks slowly, and if we were anywhere else, I'd drop to my knees and kiss it.

Damn the need to remain professional.

When Gabriella's in a good place, I tell her she can open her eyes. She starts to cry, and I'm momentarily frozen. Then she throws her arms around my neck, the stupid piece of blue tissue covering her nakedness completely forgotten.

"It's beyond beautiful," she says as I take the opportunity to rest my hands on her ass.

"I'm happy you like it," I say. "I need to wrap it for you, and I'll give you instructions on how to take care of it."

Outside my room, Ryan whistles something tuneless and I turn Gab so that her ass is out of his line of sight if he happens to step into the room. "Now, maybe you should put your panties on before I forget where we are."

"Promises, promises," she laughs, and in my heart, in that moment, I know she's the only girl for me.

When Gab's dressed and ready to go, I lead her out into the reception area. While I've been busy with her tattoo, the other artists have finished with their clients. Ryan, Darian, and Phil are all sitting around shooting the breeze. Carl's here too, catching up with shop gossip, which goes quiet as soon as they see me and Gabriella. "Did he do a good job?" Ryan asks, teasingly.

Gabriella nods. "It's perfect. He's a genius."

Carl's ice-blue eyes widen, and he nods with satisfaction. I guess it's good to hear clients are happy with the standard of the artwork around here.

"So, I'll see you soon," I say, bending to kiss Gab's cheek. She blushes when our eyes meet, conscious that we have an interested audience.

"Yeah," she says. "Thanks again."

I hold the door for her and watch her leave. When I turn back to my colleagues, they go from silent to laughing like hyenas in seconds.

"Seriously, dude. That girl has a lady boner for you and you're treating her like she's made of glass. Are you seriously not tapping that?"

"None of your fucking business," I growl.

"She's not a girl you tap," Carl says, drawing the attention of the rest of the disrespectful assholes in the place. "If you guys can't recognize wife material when you see it, I need to teach you some lessons."

"Wife material?" Ryan laughs like it's the funniest thing he ever heard.

"Yes." Carl focuses his attention on me. "You need to hold on to that one. I got a good feeling about her."

19

GABRIELLA

It's two weeks since Blake inked my skin, and my birthday tattoo has healed nicely. I don't have to wear soft, stretchy clothes anymore, and seeing it uncovered makes my heart skip with joy.

In that time, I've used the dial-a-dick WhatsApp group three times and spent time with Kain, Dalton, and Blake separately.

Kain came over in the morning before classes, and I told him my fantasy was for him to bend me over my desk and fuck me from behind. I was hoping I could keep everything tightly wrapped up in a strictly physical bow, encouraging him to be unfeeling and dominant so I could relax into his remoteness and control.

But, while the sex was like that, after, he lay on the bed next to me and kissed me so deeply and thoroughly it was as though he was trying to discover the taste of my soul.

Dalton wanted to learn another recipe, but amongst the groceries he brought with him was a lemon tart that he'd made from scratch. He fed me mouthfuls of sweet crumbling pastry and tart creamy filling that made my taste buds clamor for more.

After, I sat in his lap facing the window, and relished the way he controlled my body, even from beneath. It was easy to let Dalton take what he needed, even as I held back the part of me that wanted to sink against his big chest and never let him go.

I thought Blake would be his usual funny but slightly reserved self, hiding behind his humor so he wouldn't have to reveal what's behind the mask, but rather than pushing my boundaries physically, he wanted to be close to me. He wanted to remember sweet things from the past, memories I'd forgotten, but he could recall with clarity that painted pictures as vivid as the tattoos he inks. Even though I asked him to fuck me from behind, we somehow ended up face-to-face, his hips working into me with a slow, languid precision that felt more like relationship sex than our dial-a-dick deal. I kept my eyes closed, because staring into his beautiful gray eyes was like tumbling into a storm cloud; intense and tempestuous, filled with emotion that seemed about to rain down all over me.

I came like I was breaking open and he kissed me as though he wanted to gather up my fragments and put me back together.

And I felt myself slipping, my fingers losing a grip on the cliff-edge of my reserve, struggling to keep to the rules of the deal.

It's a Friday night and I'm standing outside Ellie's house, waiting for her to open up. It's my turn to babysit—Ellie's schedule cycles between me, Celine, Dornan, and Lara, her mom, and we're all happy to help. Noah's an easy kid. He's always asleep when I arrive and so far he hasn't woken up when Ellie, Colby, Micky, and Seb have been out of the house. They never go far, wanting to stay close enough to return in an emergency.

"There you are," Ellie says, flinging the front door

open wide and standing aside for me to enter. "I was hoping you'd get here a little earlier so we could catch up on your love life."

"My love life is nonexistent," I say. "My sex life is a different matter."

Ellie scowls as though she doesn't believe my attempts to keep the two sides apart. Maybe it's because she was wholly unsuccessful herself. "Those men were looking at you like you're a Faberge egg."

I frown, confused, as she closes the front door with a click.

"Something precious they need to take care of." she clarifies.

"They're good men," I say. "They would be like that over any human being. They've been raised right."

"Ugh," Ellie says, waving me off. "If I had time to tell you that you're an idiot, I would, but we're running late for the movies, so it'll have to wait for another day."

Colby jogs down the stairs, and Micky and Seb appear from the den. "Noah is sound asleep," Colby confirms.

"An emergency bottle of milk is ready in the fridge. Warm it up if you need it," Micky says.

"And an emergency bar of chocolate, bag of chips, and choice of soda is also available," Seb confirms with a grin.

"I'm going to hit those snacks like a rabid racoon," I laugh.

"Love you," Ellie says quickly, stuffing her arms into the sleeves of a light jacket and drawing me in for a fleeting hug.

"Love you," the men all croon in harmony.

"Yeah, get out of here," I laugh, shoving them in the backs playfully as they make their escape.

When the door is closed, I stare around my friend's home, feeling the silence rest around me like a heavy cloak.

They've been making lots of little changes, settling into their space and making it theirs as they slowly build memories. New photos have appeared on the wall beside the console table. Sweet black and white shots of them all laying on their bed, Colby on one side of Ellie, and Micky and Seb on the other. Baby Noah is cradled in Ellie's arms, and they're all beaming with zero restraint. It's a picture rooted in the trueness of their love, a picture which builds a sour lump in my throat.

It's been such a long time since I was part of a family like that. When Dad was killed in a highway accident, it was a horrendous shock to all of us. When we found out there was another woman in the car who had also perished, the shock deepened into betrayal.

It's hard for me to look at pictures of him now. I feel as though I never mourned his loss, and I know Mom is the same. The anger crystallized over all the happy memories, creating a shattered film that obscured everything that came before. Our family pictures are hidden in the back of a cupboard rather than displayed in enlarged sizes on the wall.

I look at the expressions on the faces of Ellie's men, matching their broad smiles to pictures of my family when I was a baby. There is similar joy, similar love, but it all turned out to be dark and twisted in the end.

Ellie's so content and I'm happy for her, but there's always a niggling doubt in my mind that anybody can be truly trustworthy. For Ellie, there's the added layer of complexity that her lovers are brothers. What would happen if one of them cheated? Would there be a tug of war over brotherly loyalties vs. relationship expectations? Kain and his brothers are so close, I can't imagine anything would test their connection. But what could that mean for me?

I shake my head, trying to dislodge my errant train of thought, frustrated that my mind wanders to places I've placed big walls in front of.

In the kitchen, there are more pictures from a recent vacation. I don't look too closely but focus on gathering myself a tray of treats that I can use to soothe the uncomfortable ache in my chest.

I find a true-crime drama, steering clear of Hallmark romances and chick flicks. I need to lose myself in something gripping and forget my own pathetic troubles. When my mind wanders away from the screen and back to Blake, Kain, and Dalton, I mentally run through all the reasons that we can't be together — Travis, our parents, the world, the risk that we won't stand the test of time, and everything will be broken — so much so that I convince myself that there's no hope.

But I can't push away the yearning I have for the life Ellie's made for herself. And I can't help craving the love that I know Dalton, Blake, and Kain have to give.

20

KAIN

The rumble of the crowd is audible from the locker room, setting my nerves buzzing. Coach is going over plays and I try to focus, but all I can think of is Gabriella.

She was distant when I saw her this week, like a reflection in a mirror that you want to touch but can never reach. When I gave her a ticket for today's game, she seemed reluctant to take it, but when I told her Ellie would be there to watch Dornan, she finally accepted it.

I tried not to feel offended, but when we fucked and she came like a woman possessed, there was something disconnected about her that made me ache behind my chest.

Afterwards, I don't know if she could sense my disquiet, but before I left, she rooted around in her drawer, pulling out a small button with a shamrock on it. I recognized it from a St. Patrick's Day party we'd been to when we were kids. It felt like a lifetime ago and yesterday, all at the same time. "A lucky charm," she said, pressing it into my hand. "For the game."

I brought my hand closer to my face so I could look at it. "Thanks, Gab." I slid it into my pocket, uncertain of what it meant for her to give it to me.

"Not that you need luck." She shrugged, and something about her expression made her seem defeated.

I'd left heavy-hearted, but something about that button gave me hope. She was slipping away, but there was still a part of her that wanted to reach out. That was the part I forced myself to focus on.

I turn the button over in my hand. Dornan, who must notice my lack of focus, nudges my arm. "What's that?"

"Lucky charm."

"You believe in that shit?" he asks. I know Dornan isn't superstitious. He's the one player on the team without either a fixed pregame or postgame ritual to hang on to. He breezes onto the field without a care, taking every game one play at a time. He reflects on his performance, but it's always with a level of ownership, something he could do better rather than what fate stole from him.

Maybe I need to be more like him. Less focused on fantasy and more on reality.

The button feels like a piece of Gabriella, a piece that she was comfortable to give to me. Leaving it behind in my locker might feel like a rejection of that, or it could just be me finally feeling that I'm a master of my own destiny.

I always want to be in control. It's a trait that's deeply ingrained, a part of my character that I just can't fight against. It's what I find so frustrating about my feelings for Gabriella. They're intense and head-rush inducing, like whatever will be will be. No amount of hoping for luck or relying on buttons or other superstitious trinkets is going to make any kind of difference to the way my life turns out.

When Coach is done, my teammates lumber to their feet. We do our team chant to hype ourselves up, and I quickly rest the button on the shelf in my locker.

The walk from the locker room to the field is always

accompanied by butterflies. It doesn't matter how big the guy is, how fierce his abilities, knowing how much is on the line with every game messes with a man's guts.

Knowing Gabriella is up in the stands somewhere, waiting to watch me play, makes my guts twist even more than usual. I don't want to be a disappointment to her. I want her to see me as my best. I want her to be proud.

I want her to know in her heart of hearts that I can and will do anything in my strength and power to make her happy, even if that's walking away.

But there's only so much a man can communicate on the field.

The anticipation is palpable as we're greeted by the roar of the crowd. The atmosphere is charged with energy as the national anthem echoes through the stadium, and we line up for the coin toss at midfield. Our quarterback, Alex, steps forward, ready to call the coin flip, and the tension mounts. The referee, a burly man in his forties, flips the coin, and I hold my breath as he takes his sweet time before revealing the result.

We get the advantage, and cheers erupt from our sideline. We know Coach will choose to kick off. Let the game begin.

We take our positions on the field, and our quarterback barks out orders. I ready myself for the snap, tension mounting as the ball is hiked. The back of my neck is as hot as the sun, and I feel Gabriella's eyes on me like the press of fingertips into my skin.

Football is second nature to me. I've been playing for so long that it's almost an unconscious function like breathing and blinking. Like a dance through water, tackles that happen in seconds feeling stretched out like elastic. But knowing Gabriella's out there makes everything sharper than usual.

We vie for yardage and momentum, Coach yelling

instructions from the sidelines like a man possessed, but Alex, the quarterback, keeps his head on the field. We execute our plays with precision, the sound of helmets colliding, pads crunching, and the cheers of the crowd punctuating every gain. We're dominating, gaining yards with each play, closing in on the end zone. It's so close I can practically taste it.

I'm bruised already, but that's an inescapable part of this game. Sometimes I leave the defenders grasping at air, and sometimes they floor me. Maybe Gabs can kiss me better later. The thought of her lips pressing against my ravaged purple skin makes my head swim.

Alex drops back, scanning the field for an opening. The defensive linemen charge to disrupt the play, but I'm already running, losing the defenders who've been crowding me, my legs pumping, arms ready to catch. The ball sails through the air, Alex's throw arching perfectly towards me, as if my palms are magnetized.

The crowd roars with excitement as I charge towards the goal line. I see an opening and make a sharp cut to the left, evading a tackle attempt. I'm going to do it, and Gabriella will get to celebrate my success, but before I can complete my imminent touchdown, a massive hit blindsides me. A burly linebacker from the opposing team comes at me with full force. I brace myself for impact, but the hit is brutal. His shoulder crashes into my chest, and my feet lose contact with the ground. Time slows, seconds ticking as I fly through the air, the ball slipping from my grasp.

I can't fucking breathe and when I hit with force, my head snaps forward with such momentum that I see stars.

The referee blows his whistle and I try to get up, but my head won't stop spinning. The cheers of the crowd trail off into silence, or maybe it's just my hearing. Maybe it's a concussion.

My chest feels dull, empty, my focus fades.

21

GABRIELLA

The stadium has gone deathly quiet, and I fly to my feet, straining to see, my fingernails digging into my palms so deeply I feel like I'm drawing my own blood.

Kain's down, and despite his teammates and the medical team crowding around, he hasn't gotten up yet.

"He's going to be fine," Ellie says softly, her hand touching mine, but there's a constrained pinch to her voice, a certainty wavering with doubt.

Suddenly, more people run onto the field, and the medic at Kain's side begins chest compressions. Quickly, Kain's team gather around, their big backs forming a wall around Kain, blocking the crowd's line of sight.

Ellie's arm goes around my shoulder and it's only then that I realize I'm sobbing. My fingertips are wet from my tears and my huffing, panicked breathing. "He's…what's going on?"

A man holding a large item of medical equipment is let into the protective circle and Ellie starts crying too. "That's a defibrillator, Gab. They're trying to restart his heart."

"What?" I gasp.

"His heart," she whispers again, "There's something wrong with his heart."

The words don't penetrate immediately. They linger in the air around me, somewhere outside of my mind and my heart, held there because absorbing them means knowing they are true.

The man in front of me starts explaining something about a rare condition that can occur when someone's chest is impacted hard. Something that stops a heart from beating. I hear what he's saying, a clinical explanation about a one in a million chance, and I still don't absorb what's happening right in front of me.

"I gave him a button. A lucky button." The words come out of my mouth calm, still, and quiet.

I can feel the weight of Ellie's eyes on me, her arm tightly holding me together.

"He's going to be fine," she says. "He's going to be fine."

It's those softly uttered words of reassurance that pierce the bubble, and let reality come rushing in.

"Oh god." I collapse to my seat, my breath rushing as I lose control over my body, rocking with noiseless sobs that shift everything inside me.

"Hey." Ellie sits beside me, pulling me against her awkwardly. "Gab, honey."

"The ambulance is here," the man in front says.

Ellie stands to get a better view, and she tugs roughly at my arm. "Gab…they're taking him to hospital. You should go."

"What?" I stare at her, blinking, eyes as wide as an owl's. "They won't let me. I'm not family. I'm not…"

Not what? Important?

"Here." She pulls her diamond engagement ring from her finger and slides it onto my hand. "Tell them he's your fiancé. Tell them whatever you have to. Come."

She drags me by the hand, rushing on the steps so much I fear we'll both fall. I'm light-headed with sweat blooming on my skin, fear constricting my lungs and heart so tightly that I feel like I won't make it. Ellie doesn't give up, though. We burst outside, and she frantically scans for the ambulance, finding it around a hundred feet away, parked by an emergency entrance. "Shit," she says, breaking into a run, with me still dragging behind her. A crowd of people emerges through the doors, the wheels of the gurney visible through gaps in their feet.

"Wait," she yells. "Wait."

They're loading Kain into the ambulance and Ellie forces her way between the broad shoulders of the onlooking staff. "Kain's fiancée," she yells, pushing me forward. "She'll travel with him."

Eyes drop to my hand, searching for the evidence. Coach's eyebrows raise, but he doesn't question what he's been told. "Let her in," he says.

I stumble on the step, my legs not working properly. Ellie tells me to breathe and asks me to call her from the hospital.

I nod, numb, as if I've been given anesthesia before surgery. "And call Dalton or Blake."

Coach turns to Ellie. "I've called his dad," he says. "We'll meet at the hospital."

I turn my head to where Kain is lying, hooked to machines that whir and beep, his face covered by an oxygen mask, his arm threaded with IVs. It doesn't look like him, so helpless and broken. This isn't the man that can scoop me into his arms and make love to me with the passion and ferocity of ten men. This game has broken him.

His fingers twitch, those same fingers that have given me so much pleasure, and his vulnerability hits me in the chest like a freight train. I reach out and rest my hand on the only part of him I can reach, his calf. I tell him I'm here, that he's okay, that everything's going to be fine. My voice starts out shakily but builds with strength and determination. This is a moment where I can step up or fall apart. Kain needs me to be fierce. He needs to have confidence rather than despair. I shrug off my fear and don a mask of surety.

"Kain Nowak," I say sternly, drawing the attention of the paramedic who's writing notes as we fly under blue flashing lights to the nearest hospital. "You hear me? I need you, baby. I need you. Stay with me."

His fingers twitch again, and I believe that he can hear me. "That's it, Kain. Stay with me."

I push my damp hair away from my forehead and twist so I can place both hands on his body. *Feel me,* I pray. *Feel me here with you because I don't want to be anywhere else.*

I don't know what to say to him, but I know that hearing my voice can help him remain grounded in whatever consciousness he has. "Remember when we were kids?" I ask. "When I'd toss paper airplanes into your bedroom, and you'd throw them right back?"

The paramedic smiles at me. "You guys have known each other for that long?"

I nod and he smiles, his cheeks forming dimples that make him instantly younger. "That's true love right there…"

My heart constricts and thuds like it's trying to punch me from the inside.

Love?

It's such a loaded word, filled with expectations and promises, deep as the ocean, unfathomable as the vastest plain.

I thought I didn't want it, didn't feel it, but it snuck up on me, climbing onto my back where I couldn't see it, and even though I felt its weight, I could still deny its presence.

But I can't deny it anymore. I love this man, deep in my bones, the feeling rooted to the core of me where all my memories of him as a dark-haired, blue eyed little boy who'd always wait for me when I lagged behind, live.

"Those airplanes that I used to throw, and you threw right back…I wrote inside them. I told you that I loved you so many times, but you never opened them to find out the truth. And then my dad…" I swipe at my face, frustrated by the tear that has escaped. "...I couldn't face feeling it anymore."

The beat of Kain's heart has been steady on the monitor, but now each beat creeps closer to the one before. Panic rises inside me, and I squeeze his leg harder. He has to know how I feel, right here, right now. There's no waiting, no time to sort my feelings from the list of reasons why what's grown between us is a terrible idea.

None of that matters now. Not when Kain's life is on the line. Not when I know how deep the well of loss will be if he's no longer in my life…if he's taken from me. I lean forward, squeezing his calf as hard as I can, needing to penetrate the darkness behind his closed lids. If I could put my lips on his, I would, but this is my option.

And I tell him loud and clear what's wrapped around my heart like vines of ivy.

"I love you, Kain Nowak, but if you leave me now, I will never forgive you as long as I live."

22

DALTON

When Dad comes to find me, I'm laying brick with my headphones on, blasting The Killers way too loud. He tugs out one ear pod and I notice how empty of color his usual ruddy face is. "Kain's hurt. He's in the hospital. I need you to drive me. I can't…"

We both look down at his hands, and the trembling of his fingers makes my stomach drop.

I drop my tool to the ground and wipe my hands on my trousers. "What happened?" Cold dread makes the hairs on the back of my neck prickle.

"His heart stopped, Dalton. He died on the field. They had to revive him."

"What?"

My dad stares at me, waiting for his words to register, too wrung out by worry to repeat them himself.

"Is he…?" I can't say the words.

"He's at the hospital. He's in intensive care."

"I don't understand." I realize I sound like a fucking idiot. If I was smaller than my dad, he'd probably clip me around the back of the head like he used to when I was a kid, but I'm seven inches taller than him and seventy pounds of muscle heavier.

"His heart stopped, Dalton. Just…drive us to the hospital. We need to get Blake on the way."

His voice grinds with the same bleak tone he had when Mom was nearing the end of her life, like all his energy and hope are lost.

"Let's go," I say.

I drive like I'm trapped in a nightmare, the world around me existing like a model inside a snow globe. When Blake joins us, we barely talk, lost in a world of disbelief, the fragility of life a bitter taste in our mouths. In the thirty minutes it takes us to reach the hospital, Dad receives three phone calls from Coach, updating on slight changes to Kain's health. "Thank you for being with him," Dad says on the last call as we pull into the hospital's vast parking lot.

"His fiancée is with him," Coach says over the car's speaker. "She's the one giving me updates."

"His fiancée?" Dad twists the phone from his ear to look at it, then presses it back to his ear.

"Yes. Gabriella."

"Gabriella?"

My grip on the steering wheel tightens so much my knuckles turn the color of bone. Dad's voice is high and confused and although I'm relieved that Gabriella's with Kain, the fiancée-confusion isn't ideal.

"Yes. Gabriella. Long blonde hair. You don't know his fiancée?"

"Err…of course. Sorry, the line is bad," Dad says. "We're pulling into the parking lot. We'll be there soon."

"Okay." Coach sounds relieved. Holding the fort for

the parents of a seriously ill player must be stressful.

Dad hangs up the phone and turns to me and then to Blake in the back seat. "Why is Gabriella telling people she's engaged to your brother?"

"To ride with him in the ambulance, probably." Blake finds it easier to be economical with the truth than I do. It slides from his tongue like syrup and Dad seems to relax instantly, his focus back on the road.

"I didn't know you and Gabriella were still friends," he says, his voice rising at the end like a question. "You haven't hung out in years and Travis isn't around anymore."

"We are." Blake shifts in the back seat and our eyes meet in the rearview mirror.

Friends with benefits.

I wait for my brother to embellish, but he doesn't. Sensible. Say nothing and the hole won't be deeply dug if the truth ever does come out.

I find a spot in the parking lot and we pile out of the car, making our way to the hospital entrance.

The clinical smell hits me, cloying and foreign, the reality of why we are here smacking me in the face. "There's a sign for the ICU", Blake says, pointing. We follow the directions, finding a huge gathering of football players and cheerleaders waiting outside the entrance, faces grave. Among them, Coach's gray hair and mustache stand out.

"Mr. Nowak," he says, stepping forward to greet my dad.

"Any updates since we spoke?" Dad asks quickly, his eyes flicking to the door, impatient but dread-filled.

"Nothing since then," Coach says. "I'm glad you're here. Kain needs his family around him."

"Of course."

Dad doesn't waste time with any more pleasantries. He presses the buzzer to the ICU and explains who we're here for. We're buzzed in immediately and met by a nurse in a crisp uniform. "Mr. Nowak. Kain is in a stable condition. I'll get one of the doctors to explain what has happened and the treatment he's receiving. In the meantime, you can see him but a maximum of two at his bedside."

"Is Gabriella still with him?" I ask.

The nurse nods. "She won't let go of his hand. She keeps telling him stories from the past. It's so sweet that they've known each other since they were kids. That's a real love story," she says.

Dad clears his throat, but before he can say anything, I interject. "I'll go in first, Dad. I'll get Gabriella to come out and then you and Blake can go in." He looks as though he wants to disagree but is conscious of the nurse standing in front of us.

"I'll take you through," she says.

I'm given a mask to wear and then I follow the nurse into the ICU ward. It's noisier than I expect, with machines whirring and beeping constantly. I spot Gabriella first, her head bent over Kain's body, her hand clutching his. My brother is barely recognizable, with so many tubes and wires surrounding his body. He's a big, muscular man, but in the hospital bed he seems so diminished.

I'm not a man who cries very often. Even when things are bad, there's always an internal wall that holds back any strong emotion from breaking the surface. But seeing my baby brother hooked up to machines that are monitoring his heart, knowing that his heart stopped today, is too much. My cheeks are wet and my throat burns, and I swallow reflexively, swiping at my face before anyone sees them.

"Gab," I manage to rasp. Her head whips around and as soon as she sees me, she's flying into my arms, weeping with racking sobs that are so strong, I have to hold her upright. "It's okay," I tell her. "Kain's going to be fine."

"We lost him," she gasps. "He died, Dalton. I watched him die, and they brought him back."

"Shit." I smooth her hair back from her face and take her hand in mine. She doesn't usually wear rings, but as I try to squeeze her hand reassuringly, my palm scratches on what feels like a big diamond. I raise her hand and find an engagement ring on her finger.

"It's Ellie's," she says softly. "She gave it to me to make the fiancée story more realistic."

A strange twisting feeling curls from my stomach into my chest and around my heart, but I push it aside because I need to focus on Kain. I release Gabriella and stumble towards Kain, staring down at his diminished form.

"He can hear you," Gabriella says. "I know he can. Talk to him. Let him know you're here."

I take her seat, finding it warm beneath me. I rest my hand on Kain's shoulder, words tumbling inside my skull like an eight ball, with nothing that makes any sense rising to the surface. What do you say to your unconscious brother in this situation? It's not something I'm prepared for in any way.

"Kain. Bro. It's Dalton. We're all here now. We're all here waiting for you to wake up. You're fine, bro. They're making you better, okay? They know what they're doing. The whole team is here, and Coach. And Gabriella is here too. You've just got to focus on healing, Kain. Leave everything else to us."

Gabriella rests her hand on my shoulder, squeezing gently. I cover her fingers with my own and she bends to kiss the top of my head, sending a flood of reassurance through me. I miss those small moments of affection that Mom would give me when I was a kid. She always knew when I needed a little pat on the shoulder, a kiss on the cheek, or a warm, enveloping hug. Gab is the same. She senses pain in others and knows just what to do to make it even a tiny amount better.

"I'm going to go now," I tell Kain, searching his face for a small flicker of his eyelids or movement of his lips. I see nothing. "Dad and Blake are outside, and they want to come in. I'll see you soon, okay? We're not going to leave you. We'll be here night and day until you wake up."

I rise quickly, feeling the burn of tears like there's a prickly sea urchin wedged in the back of my throat. Gabriella takes my hand, and we walk out of the ICU, shock rendering us both silent.

In the hallway, Dad waits, his arms folded around his chest as though his heart is threatening to spill over the linoleum. A doctor in his mid-fifties approaches us with a file held loosely in his hand. "Mr. Nowak," he says, and me, Dad, and Blake all answer yes. His mouth tugs at the corners, but his eyes seem apologetic, as though he's bracing himself to tell us some bad news and already feels guilty about it.

"Can I talk to you about Kain's condition?"

"Yes, of course," Dad says.

The doctor clears his throat, looking down at the floor before he meets Dad's eyes. "What's happened to him is very rare. He suffered a cardiac arrest. We believe it was due to the high-impact blunt blow he received to his chest on the field. It's incredibly rare but there's a very small window within the heart's beating cycle where, if it receives a shock, it stops beating, sending the heart into fibrillation. This is what we believe happened. His heart was restarted on the field. So far, since he's been in the hospital, he hasn't suffered another incident. That's a good sign, but he's not out of the water. When the heart is in fibrillation, it's quivering and not pumping, so blood doesn't reach the body's organs, including the brain."

"He could be brain damaged?" My dad sways on his feet and Blake grabs his arm.

"We won't know until he regains consciousness. Right now, we're keeping him sedated so his body can recover."

"I want to see him," Dad says.

I touch him on the shoulder. "Go now with Blake. I'll wait with Gabriella."

The mention of her name seems to jolt Dad from his bubble of panic. He finds her standing slightly behind me. "Gabriella?" he says.

"Yes, Mr. Nowak."

"Thank you for staying with my son."

Her arm jolts against me and when I look down at her, she burrows her face into my shoulder, overwhelmed by emotion.

"Come on, Dad," Blake says, tugging him forward. "Let's go."

I watch my dad take small shuffling steps, led by Blake, as though he's reluctant to face whatever Kain is going to look like, or maybe because the shock of today has aged him.

Turning, I pull Gabriella into my arms and try to soothe her with long sweeps of my hand over her back. She shakes against me. "He died, Dalton," she whispers against my chest. "He died in front of me."

"I know, Gab. I'm so sorry you had to see that."

She shakes her head but doesn't reply. We stand like this for a long time, two statues frozen in an embrace of fear for Kain; a brother I love.

And Gabriella?

Everything about her screams that she cares for Kain deeply, but is that just the remnants of our childhood friendship or more?

I take her hand again, touching the diamond ring on her finger.

Blake has marked her with a tattoo. She's wearing

Kain's chain around her neck. I wish it was my ring on her finger.

Ours.

The word reverberates in my head and my heart. I feel the craving for it to be true deep within me.

Now is not the time for thoughts like this. It's not the time to tell Gabriella how we all feel, but when Kain is well, and he will be well, we can't leave the deal to continue.

She needs to know what we want. She needs to know we crave to build a life with her.

But until then, all we can do is wait.

23

GABRIELLA

While Blake and Mr. Nowak spend time at Kain's bedside, Dalton and I head down to get coffee. My hands are still trembling, something that seems to be bothering Dalton a lot. He keeps lifting my hand in his and staring at it with an intense expression.

The machine produces a foamy looking concoction that I usually wouldn't touch, but under the circumstances, I clutch it in both hands, absorbing the warmth, grateful for a different focus. As I take a grateful sip, Dornan approaches, moving carefully, as though he doesn't want to invade our privacy. I guess me and Dalton must look gray with the stress of seeing Kain in such a terrible state.

"How is he?" Dornan asks.

"He's wired up to just about every machine they have," I reply, the image of Kain pricking my eyes with tears. "He's still unconscious, but that's intentional. They don't want him to get distressed. But his heart is still beating."

"Fuck." Dornan shoves his fingers through his hair, and then drops his arms by his sides, focusing on the floor in front of him.

"What the fuck happened out there?" Dalton asks.

Dornan shakes his head. "It was nothing…well, not nothing. He took a hit, but we've all taken hits like that and worse more times than any of us can count. There wasn't anything particularly bad about it. I just don't understand."

Dalton closes his eyes slowly, and I rest my hand on his elbow, feeling the frustration and hopelessness as palpable as if they were my own emotions. Knowing what caused Kain's heart to stop is something that might happen again makes it worse. "This fucking game," Dalton growls. "If it's not ankle or knee injuries, it's concussion or fucking heart attacks. It's not right."

"All sports carry risk," I remind him. "Hell, you're probably a lot more likely to pick up an injury working in construction than Kain is at football."

"Coach does everything he can to keep us safe," Dornan says, but sounds falsely bright, like an old-fashioned commercial. When he glances over his shoulder to see who's listening, our focus drifts, too. Behind Dalton, Elias is leaning against the wall looking grim. Other players are taking up the chairs, their legs spread out like giants at a kids' tea party. Coach is bent over in his seat, his head in his hands.

There's nothing he could have done differently, but that won't make him feel any less responsible. That's what being a good leader is about.

"You guys don't need to hang around," Dalton says. "I'll call Coach if anything changes, and he'll let you know."

Dornan shakes his head and widens his stance, rooting himself to the floor more firmly. "We'll be here until he wakes up."

"That could be days," I say.

Dornan shrugs. "We'll take shifts."

I touch his big arm, grateful that Kain has such good friends and relieved that he has so many people praying for his recovery.

"We should go back," Dalton says, and Dornan nods, turning to return to the rest of the team.

As we reenter the ICU, I hear my name and turn to find my mom dashing down the hallway on heels too high to make running easy. "Oh my God. Tell me Kain's okay." she gasps.

"He's okay." On hearing the news, she pulls me into a fierce hug. "Were you watching the game? Did you see what happened?"

"I saw it," I say. "It was awful."

"Oh, Gabby." She smooths my hair and pats my back, reverting to all the mom techniques she used to make me feel better in the past. Her perfume alone comforts me, and I sink against her, so grateful that she's here to support me.

But why is she here to support me? I didn't call her. Maybe Ellie did.

I draw back, resting my hands on her blouse-covered shoulders. "How did you find out what happened?"

"Lukas messaged me."

"Lukas?" My eyes immediately flick to Dalton's, finding my surprise reflected. I guess neither of us knew my mom and his dad were so close that he'd turn to her in a time of crisis.

"Okay…" I guess she notices my surprise and begins to stumble over more questions about Kain in a weirdly high-pitched voice.

"We need to go back in," I interrupt, wondering what she's going to do next. Will she take a seat with the team, or want to come through?

"I'll come in and see Lukas," she says, biting her lip the

way she does when she's nervous.

Dalton holds the door open for us, and we make our way inside the unit. As if he's expecting our arrival, Lukas appears, and as soon as he sees my mom, he seems to sag. She immediately rushes forward, wrapping her arms around him, stroking his head like she did to me only minutes earlier. And once again, Dalton and I stare at each other in shock. The way they're touching each other isn't neighborly. It's intimate. Her fingers thread through his thick black hair. His arms are wrapped so tightly around her that their bodies are pressed together from knees to cheeks.

I look down at the floor, embarrassed and confused because it looks like my mom and Mr. Nowak are lovers. Lovers who have been having a relationship and keeping it secret from their children.

"What the fuck?" Dalton whispers. "What the fuck is going on?"

"I don't know," I say. "But it looks like…"

Dalton puts his hand up as though the idea of what I am about to say is too much for him to comprehend.

I get it. While we've been skulking around living out our sexual fantasies, it looks like our parents have been doing the same thing. I want to throw up. This is so wrong on so many levels.

Lukas weeps in a way that I've never seen a man weep before, as though his heart is going to fall out of his mouth. "He died, Darly. He nearly died."

Darly?

Oh god, he has a pet name for her. Dalton reaches for my hand, and we stand like lost school children, waiting for our parents to return to help us make sense of the world. I feel like the rug has been ripped out from under my feet. I feel like I've been committing some kind of incest with Kain, Blake, and Dalton. It's ridiculous because of course that isn't the case, but no one wants to be fucking the kids of someone their momma is in a relationship with.

That's what Ellie did, isn't it?

I'm supportive of her relationship, so why am I feeling so judgmental of my own actions? Or is it that I'm judgmental of my mom? A few weeks ago, I was worried that she was lonely and all the time she was hiding a clandestine relationship from me.

"I want to go home," I tell Dalton. I need to get out of here before I say things that are hurtful and not thought through.

"I'll take you." Dalton says it without any pause, and relief washes over me. He understands. He always seems to understand me and find a way to give me what I need.

Without waiting to say goodbye, I turn and press the button to exit the unit. I don't know how Mom realizes I'm leaving but her voice calls out my name again.

I burst through the door and power walk down the hallway. Dalton doesn't follow immediately. Maybe he's talking to his dad. A hand grasps my arm, and tugs me to a standstill, and I whip around to face Mom, whose face is flushed.

"Where are you going?"

"You're fucking him?" I bark. "You're seriously fucking Mr. Nowak?"

She blanches, her head jutting backwards as though I slapped her cheek. "I'm in a relationship with Lukas. We've been dating each other for two years."

"Two years?" I screech as my brain glitches. All this time, she's been sneaking around behind my back. All this time, while I've been worried that everyone will hate me for having feelings for the Nowak brothers, my mom's been carrying on without a care for anyone else.

I can't imagine how Travis will react. He was closer to

our dad than I was. He took his death the hardest. I think that's part of the reason why he's been so protective of his friendships with Dalton, Blake, and Kain. He can't face losing anyone else important to him.

"We didn't tell you or the boys because we worried about how you'd react."

"Yeah, well. You were right to worry."

Mom pauses and inhales deeply. I can practically see her counting to ten in her head, trying to stay calm while I'm anything but. "Lukas is broken, Gabby. Neither of us can deal with this now while Kain is in a hospital bed."

"You think I can deal with it now? You lied to me. You both lied to all of us." Even as the words tumble from my lips like shards of broken glass, I know I'm a hypocrite. But I can't seem to find the balance when this is my mom, the only person I thought I could trust.

I've been holding on to that belief ever since Dad's accident. When I found out that he was a liar, I needed the surety of mom's honesty. I still do.

My foundations are rocking, Kain is sick, and I'm haunted by the guilt that my secret could smash Travis's foundations even more than Mom's will. I just don't know what to do.

And when I can't cope with my feelings, I hide away.

I turn, desperate for a place to escape to. At that moment, Ellie and Dornan walk from the direction of the restrooms.

I leave my mom, her face drawn with emotion, and grab Dornan's arm. "Can you take me home, please?"

They both stare at me, hearing my distress in the tightness of my voice. "Of course," Dornan says without hesitation. "Whatever you need."

We walk away, leaving the scattered remnants of my broken and betrayed heart trampled under my mom's feet.

24

BLAKE

The sounds of the machines are driving me fucking crazy. And the sight of Kain laid out like a corpse makes me want to punch the wall until my fist is shattered and bloody. I rub my face, and then my eyes. The dryness caused by the air-conditioned air is adding to my exhaustion and frustration. I haven't felt like this before. Completely out of control, unable to find the funny side of a situation to relieve my stress.

There's nothing funny about seeing your baby brother in a coma. There's no bright side to knowing he could have died.

He did die before they brought him back.

It's a fact I can't wrap my head around.

It's quiet now that Dalton and Dad have returned home for a shower, to get a few hours' sleep, and to gather things for when Kain wakes up. Dad said that last part so loudly it was as if he hoped Kain would hear him and spontaneously open his eyes. It was as though he believed he could will the life back into his son.

Gabriella is convinced that Kain is aware of what's

going on around him. I'm not so sure. I've been searching for signs, but there's nothing. It's like sitting next to a Resusci Annie.

All I can do is talk because that's what I do when I'm nervous. Fill the dread-laden silence with something that won't feel like it's cutting my heart in two.

It's amazing how many memories have jumped to the front of my mind so that I can recount them to Kain. Things I know would make him smile if he was awake. The pranks we used to play on Dad and Dalton with whoopie cushions and fake insects. The best one was the plastic poo we left in Dad's bed. I swear, he was apoplectic before he realized it was a joke. I laugh, but I've always felt a little bad for giving Dad such a hard time. We probably shortened his life with all our childish antics.

"Remember when you had your first kiss with Dora-Lee?" I ask a motionless Kain. "You came home looking like someone had stolen your cookie. And when I asked you what was wrong, you told me you wished you waited for it to be with Gabriella."

I sigh at the picture of us I have in my head. Kain a skinnier, younger version and me without any tattoos. Those days were filled with longing for a girl we never thought we could have. We gave up and settled for other women, passing the time and hoping that someone would measure up, but they never did.

"You got your chance, Kain. You kissed the girl of your dreams. And if you come back, you can kiss her again."

His arm twitches beneath mine and I hold my breath as I search his face for signs that he can hear what I'm saying. "She was here, Kain. She was with you the whole time, crying all over you, bro, like the state of you was breaking her heart."

I squeeze his arm. "When you wake up, we need to end this deal. We need to tell her that we want her, and nothing else will do. It'll be hard, but I don't think any of us can handle more of this halfhearted arrangement. The longer it goes on, the less real it feels. I don't know. Maybe I sound like a sentimental dick. Maybe we should all just take what we can get. But I really think she wants more from us…"

"Who wants more?" Gabriella's voice rings out and I jump so violently my ass leaves the chair. Even at first glance, I can feel the weight of distress she's carrying.

"Fuck, Gab. You trying to put me in a hospital bed too?"

"Not funny, Blake."

I stand, drinking in the sight of her. She's showered and dressed in pink yoga pants and a white oversized shirt that hangs from her left shoulder, revealing her tanned skin. With her hair pulled up into a messy bun, and her face scrubbed bare of makeup, she just radiates natural beauty in a way that takes my breath away. Beauty darkened by her concern. It's there in the shadows under her eyes and her pinched lips. "Sorry, baby. You just scared the bejesus out of me."

In two paces, I'm in front of her and I wrap her in my embrace, needing to feel her body against mine, and hoping our closeness will distract her from anything she might have overheard.

"Has he moved? Do you think he can hear us?" she asks, drawing out of the hug and staring past me at Kain.

"When I talked about you, his arm twitched."

"Really?"

She seems happy to know but distracted. There's something restless about the way her eyes are darting.

"Yeah, Gab. Of course." Her shoulders lower, and her frown smooths. "You should sit next to him." I lead her to the chair closest to Kain's head and grab another one from the adjacent wall. Silence spreads thickly between us as we keep a vigil for Kain, me desperately praying for him to heal, and Gab…well, I'm not sure what's going on in her mind.

Even when we were as close as two people can be, I still didn't feel like I could read her. It's as though she only ever wants to give a part of herself — whatever is safe — and keeps another secret part buried deep.

I take her hand, holding it on the blanket that warms my brother. "What's going on, Gab? Are you okay?"

She exhales long and low, bowing her head and closing her eyes. "Your brother is in a coma, and I just found out my mom is fucking your dad. Life's great right now, Blake. It's never been better."

"What?" I twist in my chair to face her, wondering if I heard right or if my addled brain just made up her last weird sentence out of delirium.

"My mom is fucking your dad. They have been at it for two years and kept it a secret from us because they were worried we wouldn't be able to handle it."

I splutter with laughter because it's the most ridiculous thing I've ever heard, and when Gabriella doesn't join in, I realize that she's being serious. The irony of the mess of all of our secrets dampens my laughter immediately. "You mean, we've been sneaking around behind our parents' backs while they've been doing exactly the same thing?"

"Yep."

"Shit…you don't look happy." It's an understatement. Gabriella's face is severe, and her narrowed eyes seem redder than usual.

"I can't believe she lied to me," she says, twisting the hem of her shirt between fiercely gripped fingers.

"It must be hard to hear, but sometimes people keep secrets for good reasons. Like us…"

"It's not the same thing." Gabriella sighs. "If Mom wanted a boyfriend, I wouldn't have had a problem with it. Your dad is a good man. I would have accepted it. I'm sure you all would have too."

"So, what's the problem?"

"The lying." She shakes her head and looks to the ceiling as though she'll find something that will help her cope amongst the stained ceiling tiles.

"Not all lying is the same," I tell her, keeping my tone low and easy, not wanting to provoke her and make things worse. "Like our lie, for example. We're not lying to hurt anyone. We're lying so that people don't get hurt. Isn't that the same as your mom?"

Gabriella sighs, and shakes her head, then a tear rolls down her cheek.

Fuck. As quickly as I can move, I wrap my arms around her and pull her close, kissing her forehead as she sobs. "I just…I thought I could trust her, and now it feels like there's no one in my life I can trust." Her words cut more than they should.

"What about us, Gab? You can trust us."

"Can I? You're happy lying as much as my mom."

"As much as you…" I remind her. "I would never lie to you, Gab. But I'd lie to protect you. I'd lie to keep you safe. I'd lie to keep you in my life. We'd all do anything for you, Gab. Don't you know that?"

She tips her face to mine, her forest green eyes searching. I don't know what she's looking for in my gaze. I don't know if she'll find it either. "Blake," she whispers as she sags exhausted against me.

I bend to kiss her sweet mouth, wanting her to feel how much I care for her. Wanting to let all my love for this woman linger on her lips and rest on the tip of her tongue. And she kisses me back, her tears making our sweet kisses salty. I don't know if she's accepting my affection as a balm to soothe her or just as a distraction, but for now, with everything shifting beneath our feet, it will have to be enough.

Until someone clears their throat behind us.

Gabriella stiffens, pulling away from me so quickly I unbalance and jerk forward in her wake. We both turn at the same time, finding Travis standing a few feet away from us, his eyes dark, his expression blank. It's been a while since I've seen him, and in that time he's cropped his blond hair short, and grown a light brown beard that's hardened his jaw. He's filled out too, like the environment in Germany suits him.

"Travis." I stand as my guilty heart skitters in my chest, crossing the short space between us as I would have done if he hadn't just witnessed me kissing his sister.

"Blake," he says. His voice is clipped, and his nostrils flare as he inhales a deep breath. I expect him to punch me in the face or shout obscenities about touching his sister, but he doesn't. He pulls me into a fierce embrace, banging me on the back with the flat of his hand, and I'm so stunned, I almost lose my balance against him.

"Fuck, Travis. You got here so quickly."

"I jumped on the first plane," he says. "Fuck."

I draw back and turn to face Kain, seeing what Travis is seeing. My brother, skin pallid, his chest moving in a jerky rhythmic cycle that makes him seem more machine than human.

Gab is frozen, standing with the backs of her legs against her chair, staring at her brother. She watches as Travis rests his hand on Kain's blanket-covered foot.

"Kain," he rasps. "It's me, Travis. What the fuck have you gone and done now?"

I snort, shaking my head. "Fucked himself up, that's what." My voice feels overloud, inflated by nerves.

"You've got to wake up, Kain," Travis says. "Seeing you this way is killing us. You've got so much to live for, bro. And I've just spent a fucking fortune on coming to visit, so it would be nice if you were actually awake."

We all start to laugh then, like the slightly unhinged laughter of people who are all on the brink of crying.

I tell Travis to sit where Gab was sitting, and as he makes his way around the bed, he hugs his sister. When he sits, taking Kain's hand in his own, Gabriella rests her hand on his shoulder. She's still wearing Ellie's engagement ring, but Travis doesn't notice. He accepts her comfort as he talks to Kain, searching for words that might reach him through the darkness.

And Gabriella and I stand by with fear in our hearts that when Kain wakes up, Travis won't be so forgiving and everything will shatter, driving a wedge between our families for good.

25

GABRIELLA

By the time morning comes, Kain is still sedated and me, Travis, and Blake are wrung out from no sleep and the stress of taking turns to watch Kain's heartbeat monitor, willing the next beat to come.

Dalton and Lukas return, and we swap our watch shifts, exchanging exhausted hugs and passing on the news of no change. Dalton's navy eyes are heavy with worry, the burden of being the oldest brother responsible for consoling their father resting firmly on his shoulders. Lukas doesn't appear as though he slept a wink, the shadows under his eyes cave-like in their hollowness. I need Blake to hold my hand as we leave the hospital, but he can't. Not with Travis walking slowly beside us.

We travel home in Travis's rental with an awkward silence resting between us. I can feel Travis's questions churning in his mind, and Blake's shame at having been discovered but not confronted.

And I just feel desperately sad.

Before Travis left for Germany, we were a family, and the Nowaks were our friends. The lines were clearly drawn, except they weren't. On the surface, Mom and

Lukas were neighbors who helped each other out now and again and talked about yard work and the increasing prices of everything. Travis was friends with Dalton, Blake, and Kain, and I was a mostly forgotten cling-on to their friendship where fond memories of our childhood played alongside yearnings that I kept stuffed down deep.

And everything was fine.

At least on the surface.

But now all the secrets are rising through the cracks, and I feel like we're balancing in a moment before a storm where we can see it brewing darkly on the horizon but everything around us just feels eerily empty, normality sucked into the belly of the tornado.

Back at home, Travis hugs Blake again before he leaves to go home. Blake's dove gray eyes meet mine over Travis's shoulder, searching, sad, and I swallow down my emotion and turn away, looking up at the homes that we've lived in since before we can remember, the homes that brought us together.

I follow Travis to our front door and watch him open up with his key. It's so weird to have him home, so weird how easily I got used to him not being here. Inside, the house is still, and when we close the door, a chasm forms between us. A chasm of time and all the forbidden things I've done, hoping that keeping them in a neatly contained secret deal would prevent them from causing hurt.

Funny how our lies always come back to bite us on the ass.

"So, you're with Blake now?"

The shock of his outright question forces me back a step. I inhale and exhale quickly, my eyes focusing on a spot on the floor. I can't deny what he saw. I can't pretend it didn't happen.

But I could lie. Pretend it was a one-off, the result of sadness about Kain. I could tell him I needed comfort and

Blake was there. Except that makes Blake sound like an opportunist. It makes Blake sound like a man who'd take advantage of me in my lowest moment, and that's not who he is at all.

I could lie, but with Travis's narrowed blue eyes fixed on me, his brows like serious slashes on his face, I can't think through the impact of an untruth. I can't weave a realistic sounding fantasy where I haven't been having sex with all of his best friends.

"I've been fooling around with all of them," I blurt, bringing my hands to my heated face and hiding away from the probable horror in his expression. Seeing disappointment or anger in his eyes would be too much when I'm barely holding myself together.

"All of them." There's no question in his voice. Those three words come out like a statement of fact. As though he's reading a menu and telling me that sea bass with crushed potatoes and green beans is on the special's menu.

"I know you read my diary," I say, still cowering. "I know you know how I feel about them."

"And how do they feel about you?"

Peeking over my fingers, I find Travis leaning against the wall, looking so much like my dad before he died that I cringe. What would Dad think about what I'm doing with my brother's best friends? He wouldn't like it. He probably would have called me all the names under the sun, even though that would have made him a hypocrite.

"I don't know," I say. "They treat me well. We made a deal…a no-strings arrangement."

Travis sighs and shakes his head. "I leave for a couple of months and…"

"Mom's in a relationship with Lukas Nowak," I blurt. "She told me yesterday…it's been going on for two years."

He pushes off the wall and runs his hand over his head. He used to have such thick blond floppy hair but now it's so short it's hardly visible, like a layer of sun-kissed velvet. "I'm too tired for this," he admits. "I need to sleep."

"Mom's still renovating your room," I tell him. "It's a mess of paints and dust sheets."

"Guess I'll sleep in her room," he says, already climbing the stairs. Staring after him, I feel as though all my self-respect has liquified and slid down inside me, pooling in my feet. Even though I'm a fully grown woman who's comfortable in my sexuality, I still hate feeling like my brother is disapproving of my actions. I wish he'd shout at me. Tell me all the reasons why I'm making a mistake. Tell me to break off the deal with his friends and live like a nun until I find a husband. Anything but retreating to sleep.

I get it though. With Kain still so sick, all of this seems so unimportant. Sex is barely a shadow when it comes to the monolithic nature of death.

"I love them," I whisper as he's turned the corner. It slips out of my mouth and hangs in the air around me like mist on a winter morning. The truth laid bare, uttered out loud before I've even admitted it to myself. "And I think they love me," I add, because I believe it's true. I really do. But none of it matters. Not really. Because a house built on shaky ground is destined to crumble.

26

DALTON

"We're going to reduce his sedation," the doctor explains, his dark, serious eyes drifting to Kain and then back to me and Dad. "It's a slow process, so don't be daunted if he doesn't regain consciousness immediately. He may also be very confused, perhaps delirious. That won't indicate the presence of any damage. He's been through a lot and even if everything is fine, it may take him a while to get back to normal."

My dad takes a shuddering breath and lowers himself back into his seat that has rested next to Kain's head for as many hours as he's been able to take. The sounds of the machines and Kain's stillness are hard to bear, and Dad is mentally exhausted.

If Mom was here, things would be different. She'd be the one crying and worrying and Dad would be behind her, providing strength and reassurance. He's good at that role.

Instead, I rest my hand on his shoulder, hoping it'll provide him with some comfort. It's been hard to see him cope with so much pain. Harder because I'm suffering too. I haven't slept well since Kain's injury. At best, I manage three hours before I wake with a racing heart and wild sense of panic. Some nights it's an hour and then I lie awake turning over all the possible outcomes, feeling helpless, praying harder than I've ever prayed for my baby brother to wake and be in one piece.

"He's going to be fine," I say, as much for Dad as myself, but it sounds like stupid over-claim, and I wince when one of the nurse's concerned eyes meet mine.

Watching the medical team work to switch out IVs, removing one type of drug and adding another has my heart wrapped in barbed wire. I try to focus on Kain's face, willing the first movement of his eyes, the first flicker of his eyelids, his first recognition of us by his side.

I send a quick message to Blake, Gabriella, Travis, and Coach to let them know what's happening. Their support through this has been amazing. The team has been present outside every day, working in shifts, keeping a vigil for Kain's recovery.

"Kain," Dad rasps, making me jump. "We're here. When you're ready to open your eyes, we're waiting."

All we can do is wait.

It's not a quick process. The doctor was right. Gabriella messages every ten minutes asking for updates. I tell her I'll confirm as soon as he's woken up, but she's impatient and decides it's time to return to the hospital, even though she only left four hours ago and hasn't slept yet.

I finish a response, urging her to be careful on the road when Dad's hand clutches at my arm. "His eyes moved," he hisses. "Look."

Kain's eyes flicker as though he's blinking but with his lids closed. His lips part as he inhales a long breath. The doctor watches, jotting down notes, but I can't absorb anything else that's happening because I'm so focused on

Kain.

Dad reaches for Kain's hand, taking it in his and squeezing. "Son," he says. "It's okay. Everything's okay. You're fine. I'm here. Dad's here. Wake up."

I swallow thickly, the pleading in my father's voice too much for me to handle. People say that you don't understand how much your parents love you until you have a child of your own, but I know. My father has aged ten years. He'd cut out his own heart and stuff it into our chests if it meant we'd live.

Kain's fingers move in Dad's fierce grip and Dad almost jumps out of his skin, staring down as though he can't quite believe it's really happening. He turns to me, his mouth open, tears streaming down his cheeks. "Look, Dalton. Look."

"I can see, Dad. I can see."

Resting my hand on his shoulder again, I watch as Kain moves his head slightly and scrunches his brow. For a second, his expression is so serious and Kain-like that I almost laugh. He's in there. My brother is still in there.

I know the doctor told us to be patient, but I'm not. I want to shout from the rooftops that my brother is waking up. I want to grab him by the shoulder and shake him into consciousness until he says something in his humorless way that always makes me laugh.

We're not just brothers. He's a part of me and I'm a part of him and if anything happened to him…took him away…a part of me would be taken too.

His eyelids flicker again, this time revealing a hint of white and the crystal blue that I've missed so much. As if his eyelids weigh two-hundred pounds, he can't seem to lift them.

"Kain," Dad pleads again. "Come back to me, son. Open your eyes."

And as if all he needs to hear is the reassurance of our

father, Kain's eyes finally open.

I crowd in closer with Dad. "We're here, Kain," I say as he blinks, gaze drifting, expression impossible to read. "We're here. You're okay. You're in the hospital. There was an accident, but you're okay now. You're okay."

Kain blinks again, confusion lowering his brows, his tongue pushing between his dry lips to wet them.

Dad turns to look at me again, uncertainty clouding, worry twisting, desperation clawing in his eyes.

My heart feels like a drop of water falling into an echoing cave and I can't breathe.

Will he be okay?

Please be okay.

"Dad," Kain whispers. "Dad." And Dad crumbles, face falling into Kain's open palm, kissing my brother's hand over and over until I have to walk away and brace myself on the window ledge before I crumble too.

He's awake, I message to everyone who loves him. *He's awake.*

Now all we have to do is wait to see what damage has been done.

27

KAIN

"Kain, it's time to take your meds." A hand rests on my shoulder, squeezing slightly, and I rouse from sleep, feeling groggy and delirious. I have no idea what day it is or what time. It's been that way since they slowly brought me out of the induced coma and removed the ventilator. At least, that's what they told me they did. My mind can't seem to grasp onto what is reality and what are dreams from the period of unconsciousness. Everything is weirdly surreal.

I clear my throat, wincing at the soreness there. The doctor told me it will take a while to heal. It's what happens when a person is intubated quickly. "Water," I rasp and the nurse presses on the button on my bed to raise my head. She's ready with a small potful of tablets and a glass of cool water. Just the thought of having to swallow those small, white chalky blocks makes me shudder. My whole body feels sore.

"What time is it?" I croak, taking the water. "It's midnight, sweetie," she says. "You've slept so much today."

"I feel like I got hit by a train."

"You might as well have," she laughs. "That bruise on

your chest is all colors of the rainbow."

I'm wearing a scratchy hospital gown that's fastened at the back, but I try to open the neck to look down at my body. Even in the darkness under the gown, what she's talking about is evident.

"Where is everybody?" I ask. The last time I was awake, Dad and Dalton were here. They told me that Gabriella and Blake had been taking shifts, and that my whole team was camping out outside the hospital. Travis is here, too. Back from Germany.

"I sent someone out while I did my checks, but he'll be back."

She makes notes while I work through the tablets, gnawing on her lips as she focuses. She must be in her mid-fifties. It's reassuring to be in the care of someone who seems so experienced.

I flex my feet, relieved that they can move. Even though the doctors have confirmed that everything seems okay, I'm still not one-hundred-percent certain. My body doesn't feel my own, and my mind is a tangle of confusion.

"Well done," the nurse says, taking the now empty tablet pot.

"I didn't do much," I croak.

"You did what you needed to do. Do you want to lie back down?"

I shake my head. "I've slept enough."

She takes the control pad that works the bed and rests it next to my hand. "If you change your mind."

"Thanks."

She nods and leaves, bustling away to deal with another poor soul trapped in this place. I'm grateful for the care but I want to get out of the hospital as soon as I can. Getting well in a place surrounded by sickness takes a whole ton of mental strength. The machines around me are reminders of what I could potentially slip back into.

Travis appears a couple of minutes later, probably given the all-clear by the nurse.

"You're awake," he says, grinning and making his way around to my bedside.

"And you're back from Germany." I'm sure we've already had this conversation, but I can't remember.

"I came as soon as I heard about your amateur dramatics."

"Funny," I choke, laughing. "This shit doesn't feel amateur." I let my hand hover over my bruise and Travis winces on my behalf.

"You gave us all a fucking scare, man. I…" He pauses, swallowing thickly. "I couldn't believe it when Dalton called me. I thought he was joking. I actually laughed."

"I don't blame you. This shit is fucked up."

"It is. I mean, we're young, aren't we? Too young to deal with this."

"Exactly." I flex my fingers at my sides, wanting to check they're still working, too. When the doctor talked to me about the risk of cerebral damage from lack of oxygen, I freaked out. But so far, the tests all look good. And despite feeling like I got trampled by a herd of buffalo, my mind seems to be my own. "Where's your sister?"

"I had to fight her to leave. She's got a big assignment to do, and she needs sleep."

I draw my bottom lip between my teeth and Travis's blue eyes, that are a match to his sister's, scan my face.

"She told me, Kain."

"Told you what?"

"What y'all have been doing."

I lower my lids as the heat of shame colors my cheeks. "I…" What the hell do I say? I'm sorry for banging your sister? I'm sorry for betraying you? Sorry doesn't cut it in this situation. Getting on my knees at Travis's feet and begging for forgiveness wouldn't cut it.

"How do you feel about her?" Travis asks.

"I love her," I blurt before I have a chance to think through the impact of such a statement. But even with those three monumental words hanging between us, I don't regret saying them for a minute. "I think I've always loved her."

Travis nods his head once, cataloging an important response and evaluating it to see if it measures up. That he hasn't punched my lights out is a miracle.

"And Blake and Dalton?"

I blow out a breath through pursed lips, the magnitude of his questions hitting me hard in the chest. Can I speak for my brothers about such an important question? Should I?

"They love her too, Travis. I'm sorry we didn't come to you before. We should have had the guts to tell you how we felt and ask for your opinion. We were cowards."

He nods, and then his face splits into a grin. "You think I didn't know how you felt? You think I'm blind, Kain? I was there all those days we spent together. I used to see you, Blake, and Dalton looking at Gabriella like she was Aphrodite, rising from the waves. I used to see her sideways glances at you all, blushing whenever you came around. All that tension…" He shakes his head and whistles. "Why do you think I told Blake about her diary? I wanted you to know she liked you. I wanted my sister to have a chance to be loved by someone I thought would be worthy of her."

"Are you serious?" I blink back tears, finding that my time in a hospital bed has made me an emotional wreck.

"I'll admit, I thought she'd pick one of you rather than all three. Though I should have realized there might be a chance she'd end up with all of you when Ellie hooked up with her stepbrothers."

"All this time, we've been feeling guilty as hell for keeping everything secret."

He rests his hand on my arm, squeezing. "Kain, you guys are like my brothers. You'll always be my brothers from another mother. I trust you with my sister, and I know you'll love her the way she deserves."

"We will," I say. "There's just one problem."

"What's that?" Travis asks.

"I'm not sure if she feels the same way."

28

GABRIELLA

Kain's been awake for two weeks and has been recovering well. During that time, his father has barely left his side during the day, and when I've tried to visit at night for some alone time, there's always been someone from the team or his extended family visiting, too.

It's been impossible.

My heart is bruised and there are so many things unsaid between us that he almost feels like a stranger.

Travis isn't angry with me. He isn't angry with Mom either. It's like he went to Germany one man and returned another. Even though I've asked him about his adventure, he hasn't told me anything personal, just rambled on about the building he works in and his colleagues, and the differences between Germans and Americans.

I want to know what made him the way he is now. I can't work out whether he's stuffing down his anger because of what happened with Kain or if he genuinely has returned as a philosophical, chilled, mature man. Half of me is worried that he's going to explode once Kain is home, and the other half is petrified that he won't question this relationship...and then what?

I have to admit my feelings.

Or I risk Dalton, Blake, and Kain walking away because it was always only supposed to be temporary.

Neither option is what I want.

I've been avoiding spending any time alone with Mom, and the distance that has formed between us feels weird and sad. I'm adrift with no anchor. It's as though there is a wall between me and everyone I used to be connected to.

I've even been avoiding Ellie and Celine, too. Their questions will make me face things I'm not ready to deal with.

I'm a terrible daughter, a terrible sister, a terrible friend, and a terrible lover.

In the day, I dedicate myself to assignments and extra reading, and at night I fight my thoughts by falling down the TikTok rabbit hole, until I'm bleary-eyed and my mind is desperate to switch off.

But today Kain is leaving the hospital, and everyone is on edge. Mom's been baking since early this morning and the whole house is scented with her famous gooey chocolate cake. We've been invited to the Nowaks for dinner and Dalton messaged me last night to request that I arrive earlier than Mom and Travis. It'll be the first time we'll be alone together since before Kain's injury and my stomach is a ball of frantic moths searching for their escape.

I'm ready to leave, dressed in a pretty white dress with tie straps and embroidery anglaise detailing, my hair loosely curled and pinned, and gold gladiator sandals strapped up my legs. I've even painted my fingernails and toenails in a matching shade of baby pink. When I glance at myself in the mirror, I bite my lip, realizing I've subconsciously dressed myself up like a bride or maybe a Greek goddess. It's too late to change, though, so I grab my purse, hoping no one else will notice, and jog down the stairs. If I'm quick, I can just call out my goodbyes and make a speedy, uneventful exit.

It doesn't work out that way.

"Gabriella," Mom calls. "Can you come in here for a second, please?"

I feel like I got a D on my report card, and I am about to get a grilling.

In the kitchen I find Travis at the table focused on his phone, and Mom grating white chocolate over an almost finished cake. She looks up, smiling when she sees me out of my usual yoga pants and baggy tees. Then her expression changes. "I think we should talk before we go next door. There's a lot that's been brushed under the carpet while Kain has been recovering and I don't want it to come out while we're guests at someone else's house."

I nod even though I'd rather just leave everything under the carpet, even our elephant sized secrets and lies.

"We haven't spoken about me and Lukas since the hospital. I wanted to say that I'm sorry I didn't tell you that we're in a relationship. I should have been honest but opening it up to all the potential conflict just didn't feel right. It's been a long time since either of us has been happy and it felt fragile. Do you understand?"

It's hard to find words to answer because I don't want to sound like a spoiled brat and I don't have a leg to stand on when it comes to keeping secrets, but I'm still sad and I still feel betrayed.

If I was ten, the kind of outburst that's brewing inside me would be excusable, but I'm an adult now. I have to fight for maturity to deal with adult issues. Instead of yelling, I try to convey my feelings in a measured tone.

"When Dad died, and we discovered his secret, it really shook my trust," I say, watching Mom's face lose color. Travis finally lowers his phone and focuses on me. "We didn't ever talk about it as a family. I feel like none of us processed what happened…finding out that he'd been lying and his death. I had no place to put my anger or my feelings of betrayal. I didn't want to upset either of you by bringing it up. We all brushed that time under the rug, and it has sat between us for so long."

Mom opens her mouth to speak, but I put my hand up. I'm on a roll now and I don't want to be interrupted.

"When I found out you'd been lying too, it touched a nerve, Mom. You've been the only person in my life that I've ever fully trusted and now, I feel like that's gone."

"I didn't ever lie," Mom says. "I just wasn't open about the truth."

"Semantics," Travis says, and we both turn to stare at him.

"Is this how you feel too, Travis?" Mom asks.

"Yes," he says, placing both hands flat on the table. "Well, the stuff about Dad. Keeping Lukas a secret doesn't bother me as much as it seems to bother Gabriella. I just want you to be happy. I've been away and I've been worried about both of you here. Now I find out that the Nowaks have stepped in to take my place."

"No one could ever take your place, Travis," I say, shocked.

He shrugs, which is a blatant brush-off, but I'm not standing for that. Not now.

"No one will ever take your place," I repeat, moving to sit next to him. I put my arm awkwardly around his shoulder and inexplicably he leans into me, wrapping me in the kind of hug we've never really been comfortable with before.

"They love you, you know," he whispers in my ear. I jolt back, his words stinging my heart.

"What?"

"Kain told me," he says. "If you want them, it's up to

you."

I stare into my brother's eyes, searching, desperate to know he's okay with what he's saying. He's a good man. Unselfish and stoic. He'd bear what made him unhappy if he thought it was what I wanted. "And your friendship?"

"They're my brothers. Maybe they'll become my brothers-in-law." His smile is rye, but his eyes are sparkling.

"Trying to marry me off already," I snort.

"What's going on?" Mom asks. "What have I missed?"

"I'll leave Travis to fill you in," I say, rising and checking my watch. I'm already running late. "See you later."

Before Mom can object, I'm striding from the house, those terrified moths morphing into excited butterflies. They love me. Kain confessed it to my brother, his most trusted friend, before he admitted it to me. I can't be mad about it, though. They admitted it to Travis before I had the courage to accept the reality of my feelings.

As I walk the path between our houses, I recall skipping this way wearing my best flowery yellow summer dress, my hair in braids tied with ribbon, and yellow ballet pumps on my feet. Our parents were taking us to the local fair, but I was impatient to wait for the time we were all leaving. I wanted to show Dalton, Blake, and Kain my new dress. I wanted them to see how pretty I was.

The lump in my throat is large as I remember them in their button-down shirts and dark jeans, hair brushed to the side, faces glowing from the scrubbing their mom must have given them. Their eyes had widened when they saw me, and I knew it was because I looked nice. I looked different from the scrappy Gabriella who tagged along on all their escapades. I looked like a princess, and their appreciative gazes had made me feel so special.

When Dalton opens the front door, his eyes widen in

just the same way as all those years ago, drinking me in like I'm an iced drink and he's desert parched.

"Gabriella," he breathes, reaching for my hand and drawing me into an embrace that's tighter than it should be. "You look…"

I beam up at him, reaching out to caress his thick black beard, the solid column of his neck, his bulky shoulders that speak of power and capability. "I missed you," I say, watching his eyes soften and his body relax with relief.

"I missed you, too," he breathes. "So much."

And the sound of his voice, low and gravelly just for me, sends heat right through me. I have to bury my face into his warm shirt that smells of the ocean on a clear fall day and grip him as tightly as he hugged me. We stand that way, framed by the open doorway for longer than I've ever been held by Dalton, and I never want him to let me go.

When he eases his hand from my back to push the door, Blake's voice calls out, "Is she here?" before he appears at the top of the stairs.

Dressed in a tight gray shirt that shows off his lean muscular frame and the swirls of ink that stretch down his arms, Blake looks ready for a fight, but his smile tells another story. That smile that illuminates his face speaks of fun and laughter and humor that can make even the saddest day lighter. His brown hair flops over his forehead as he nears, and he pushes it back impatiently. I'm drawn into his embrace as soon as he's close enough to reach me, and kisses are pressed first to the crown of my head, then my forehead, then my nose and finally my lips. I'm swept into the whirlwind of his affection and never want to return to the ground.

"You're a sight for sore eyes," he says, gripping me by the upper arms and looking me over. "That dress is…" He leaves a shake of his head and his raised eyebrows to communicate his appreciation. It works well enough to make me blush.

I touch his stubbled cheek, watching his lids lower in satisfaction. "I missed you," I tell him, not wanting him to hear anything different from his brother. We are in this together, and that will require a level of fairness.

"Where's Kain?" I ask.

"Dad went to collect him from the hospital. He's desperate to come home. Poor guy is sick of hospital food."

At the mention of food, the delicious aroma in the air registers. "What's on the menu?"

Dalton grins, and the soft skin above his thick beard flushes an adorable shade of pink. "Come see." He takes my arm and leads me into the kitchen. Laid out on a trestle table is a hot plate with several warming dishes covered with aluminum foil. On the counter there are numerous large bowls filled with Greek salad with crumbly white feta cheese, a potato salad with celery and finely chopped scallions, a pasta salad with sun-dried tomatoes and olives and what looks like a homemade focaccia bread with rosemary. I step forward to peek beneath the wrap of the hot dishes, finding spiced chicken, a casserole in a rich sauce, and a spicey rice. Everything smells mouthwateringly delicious.

"You did all this?" I ask Dalton, my gaze flicking between him and Blake, who's leaning against the doorjamb with his arms folded and a smile curving his kissable lips.

"I did," Dalton says.

"He wouldn't let any of us in here. Not even for a glass of water."

"What does your dad think?"

Dalton folds his arms, determination lowering his brow. "I told him I want to become a chef…own a restaurant one day."

I straighten, smoothing my hands over my dress. "Are

you serious? You really told him?"

"I did." Dalton reaches for me, tugging me forward and kissing me gently on the lips. "If it wasn't for you, Gab, I never would have found this thing that I love…I never would have been brave enough to take this step."

"What did he say?"

"I think he could see I wasn't going to hear a word against it." Dalton's fierce determination about his new direction in life is evident in the way he stands, the way he talks, the way he moves. I don't think I've ever seen him like this.

"That's amazing," I say, my swell of pride heating my skin.

Blake nods his agreement. "Finally, he can stop bitching and boasting about how hard his job is."

"I don't know," I say, touching Dalton's ropey forearm. "Chefs have it tough, especially the ones who are training."

"Don't encourage him, Gab."

I grin and we all laugh, Dalton's excitement about his future filling us with a contagious buoyancy.

"Kain is changing his path too," Blake says. "He'll tell you more himself."

I stare at Blake, waiting for him to tell me more. Kain isn't in any position to be thinking about the future. He needs to fully recover first, and that's going to take some time.

Blake's hands go up, and he steps into the room. "He's decided to drop out of the team."

"He has?" The relief I feel is so visceral, it makes my knees weak. After watching him drop like a stone on the field, I don't think I would ever be able to face attending another game or knowing he was out there in danger.

"The doctors told him they could sign him off to play

again, but that there is an increased risk of him having issues in the future. His heart was bruised. Kain's decided he'd rather live a long life than take a risk for football."

"And he's going to work with Dad…take on all the business side…when he's finished studying." Dalton says. There's relief in his voice and I realize that this is part of the reason Lukas has let him go and follow his dreams without a fight.

"He always did want to go into business," I say.

"Yeah, but not the family business." Blake rubs the back of his neck. "A lot has changed."

"What about you?" I ask. "Do you have any bombshells to drop?"

Blake shakes his head, then shrugs his left shoulder. "Anything I have to say shouldn't be a surprise."

I stare at him, waiting for more, but the sound of a key turning draws all our attention.

When Kain walks through the door, taking each step slowly, I can't hold myself back. I rush toward him, so relieved to see him on his feet, overwhelmed by how much older he looks with his full beard, worried by the hollows that remain beneath his beautiful blue eyes. My arms envelope him before he has a chance to respond, pinning his arms at his sides. Tears I didn't know were coming stream down my face.

So much relief pours out of me, my knees shake, and my body is wracked by sobs that turn into relieved laughter. "You're back." I say, my words muffled into his shirt.

"I'm back." His voice is gruff with emotion as he eases his arms from my tangled embrace and holds me against this body. He feels different; slimmer, maybe. The time he spent in the hospital has robbed him of his training bulk, but he's still solid and so much bigger than me that he makes me feel safe and protected, even in his diminished state. The kiss he presses to my forehead is chaste, like a brother would give a sister, and I remember that Lukas is behind him, closing the front door, relieved to have his son safely home.

There are so many things I want to say to them all, but this isn't the time. We've had years to build up to this moment. Years to get to know each other, years to develop feelings. To want to rush things now is selfish, but I can't help myself. A switch has flicked for me. Hearing Travis giving his blessing and hearing confirmation that they love me, it's everything I need. It's allowed me to relax enough and to accept what I want, what I feel.

The doorbell rings, and when Lukas opens the door, Mom and Travis greet the Nowaks, stealing Kain away from me with happy relief at his recovery.

I walk back into the kitchen, half in a daze. Everyone is so happy; the air feels alive with it. Lukas steers Mom with a gentle hand on the small of her back. Travis greets his buddies with quick, sharp embraces, and a wide smile. Everyone gushes over Mom's welcome home cake, and then Dalton's food, and I stand back and observe these people who I love, and who love each other.

And it doesn't feel wrong to me that I love Dalton, Blake, and Kain anymore. It feels like I've arrived home from a journey that's lasted a whole lifetime.

We fill our plates with food, and moan over the deliciousness. We listen to Kain talk about his recovery and how grateful he is to be at home. Dalton rests his hand on my thigh, a possessive and reassuring action that keeps me grounded, and everything feels so perfect, I have to swallow back tears.

I catch Mom staring at us all with a soft smile on her face. I guess Travis told her everything. I guess she's not going to give me the same kind of grief I gave her about her choices. Lukas is the last to know, and maybe his reaction will be different, but as Blake finds my hand beneath the table and Kain's gaze slides to mine, filled with love and heat, I feel sure we can accomplish anything, as long as we're together.

29

DALTON

Kain's welcome home dinner is received so well that I feel overwhelmed. Preparing and cooking so many dishes was hard work but more fun than I've ever had in my day job. Not only has it cemented my desire to cook, but it's made me realize that without a true passion, life can become dull and uninteresting.

Nothing about my life feels like that now.

Darleen insists that she will wash the dishes with Dad while the rest of us relax in the den. As Kain makes the short but slow walk to Dad's recliner, I catch Travis's gaze drifting to each of us, a small smile tugging the corners of his mouth. "I'm going to head off," he says.

"No." Gabriella reaches to touch his arm. "Stay. It'll be fun."

"I have to catch up on work," he says. "I didn't get time off to come home. I've had to bring my project with me, and with the time difference, getting in touch with the colleagues I need information from isn't easy. This was cool, though. It's good to see Kain home safe and sound. It's been good to spend time with you all."

"When are you going back?" I ask.

"I don't know," Travis admits. It's the first time he's mentioned an uncertain return date. Something about the way he says it makes me wonder if he's intending on going back to Germany at all.

"We'll hang out tomorrow?" Blake says. "Maybe grab a beer."

"That'll be great," Travis says. "Maybe I'll book to come see you for some ink."

Blake beams, the prospect of inking another one of his friends and family like an affirmation of his talent.

Gabriella leans in to kiss her brother and hold him in a sisterly hug, then he shakes each of our hands and I accompany him to the door. "Mom knows about you guys," he says as he pauses on our front step. "She knows you're good guys, so even though it's not a standard arrangement, she knows you'll take care of her daughter."

"You serious?"

He nods and shoves his hands into his pockets. There's something different about Travis since he returned from Germany. A sadness that I can't quite put my finger on. He smiles, but it doesn't quite reach his eyes. He's with us, but he still feels apart.

"And you?" I ask. "Are you okay with it?"

"I told Kain I am."

"You don't know how much it means to us for you to give your approval."

He shrugs, brushing off my comment, but it is a big deal. Bigger than he seems to realize.

"Just look after her," he says. "That's all I expect, okay?"

"Of course. That's all we want to do."

He turns and takes another step. "I'll see you tomorrow." He calls it over his shoulder and doesn't turn to wave. I watch as he makes his way next door with rigid shoulders, and my stomach tightens. I won't discuss it in front of Gabriella, but when she leaves later, I'll tell my brothers. Something's not right with our friend and we need to find out what it is.

Back in the den, Kain's eyes are drooping, and Gabriella is watching him, concerned. "I think you need to go to bed," she says, rising and taking his hand so that he can't say no. Kain uses his other hand to push himself up, and wobbles slightly on his feet, requiring Gabriella to wrap her arm around his back. "You overdid your first day home."

"I'm fine," he says quietly, even though it's quite clear she's right.

Blake stands quickly, stepping in to support Kain's weight. I closely follow as they make their way upstairs, bracing to catch Kain if he loses his balance. Thankfully, he makes it up okay.

In Kain's bedroom, Blake helps him to sit on the edge of his bed. Gabriella kneels before him, peeling his socks from his feet. There's so much tenderness in the way she touches Kain, as though she's worried he might break. He watches her, conflicted. I know my brother and he won't like being seen as weak and helpless, but he will enjoy Gabriella taking care of him. It's been a long time since a woman laid tender hands on us. "Lay back," she says, helping him twist until his legs are on the bed and his head is cradled by his pillow.

"Come lie with me," Kain says softly, patting the bed next to him. Quickly, Gabriella crawls into the nook between his arm and chest, snuggling against him. Her hand hovers over his chest as though she remembers how bruised he's been there and doesn't want to risk touching him. His hand reaches out to grasp hers and presses it to his heart. "It's okay," he says. "I'm not going to break if you touch me."

I sit on the bed on one side, and Blake matches me on the other. It's the first time we've all been together with any privacy for weeks. It's been too long.

"I…I thought I was going to lose you," Gabriella whispers, her voice sounding constricted. "I thought that…"

"I'm okay," Kain says. "You don't need to go back there now. We need to look forward."

I rest my hand on my brother's leg, wanting him to know I understand. He's faced his mortality and doesn't need to be reminded of it. He needs positivity and things to look forward to. We all need to remember that in the weeks and months to come.

"I thought that I was never going to be able to tell you that I love you," she says.

Kain twists to stare down at her. "Say it again," he rasps, emotion drawing his features.

"I love you," she whispers. "I love you all."

Kain kisses her mouth fiercely, as though her confession has made him regain strength, and Gabriella kisses him back, gripping the sleeve of his shirt in her fingers until her knuckles are white and small moans reverberate in her throat.

My heart swells, feeling her words in a place that has hoped for them for so long and never believed they would come.

"We love you too, Gab," Blake says, resting his hand on her waist. She turns, flushed from Kain's kiss, and draws Blake closer until they're eye to eye, mouth to mouth, kissing passionately.

My heart soars, feeling the shift between us. The deal we struck is slipping away, and in its place is something deeper that will unite us. Kain turns to embrace Gabriella from behind as Blake worships her from the front. I clamber onto the bed, waiting for Blake to release her, needing to show her just what her words — her love — mean to me.

When Gab draws away from Blake, she searches for me and reaches her hand out as I climb over her. The embrace she gives me is as tight as the one by the front door, but this time she whispers, "I love you, Dalton," into my ear and I have to kiss her. My brothers give me space to settle between her thighs and I take her mouth, murmuring words of affection between nibbles of her lips and cheeks and jaw. She smells so good and feels like home, and it's all I can do to stop myself from ripping off her clothes and taking her right here, right now.

When I draw back, Gabriella whimpers, her hips shifting against the bar of my rock-hard cock, searching for pressure. I thrust once, twice, giving her hints of what is hers now. What will always be hers as long as she wants it.

"Damn, you're needy," I smile, pushing her hair back from my face.

"I think our girl needs some good loving," Kain rasps, his fingers twirling in her hair that fans across the pillow like spun gold.

"I think our girl needs some dial-a-dick," Blake says, and we all laugh so hard that tears form in our eyes.

"Not to put a damper on the dick idea," Kain says, "But Dad and Darleen are currently downstairs, and my heart isn't ready for the kind of dicking Gabriella deserves."

Gab turns and reaches out to touch Kain's face. "Then we'll wait, baby," she says. "My vibrator hasn't had any action recently. It can keep me going for as long as you need."

Both me and Blake scowl at that idea, but Gab makes a tutting sound with her tongue. "It's either all of us or none of us from now on. If this thing is going to work, we need to be united."

"She's right," Blake says. "I fucking hated knowing when you guys were over there making Gab feel good and I was over here or at work imagining it."

"Me too," Kain says. "Although watching you guys through the window was hotter than Satan's BBQ."

"Watching is fine," Gab says. "In fact, watching is horny as fuck."

"That's our girl," I laugh, kissing her again fiercely.

She turns to Kain, touching his bearded jawline. "I know you're not ready for the main course, but how about I give you a little starter?"

He reaches down and squeezes his cock. "I think I could handle that."

I draw back and give Gab space to change position. She tugs at Kain's black joggers and underwear, revealing his cock. She turns to me and Blake, her eyes gleaming. "One of you needs to listen out for the parents. Tonight you get to watch. If the parents stay downstairs, you'll get your turn. If not, next time, I'll give you starters, main course, and dessert."

"Shit," Blake says, licking his lips with anticipation.

I decide to take door duty, not trusting Blake to keep his concentration when he's watching Gabriella suck Kain into oblivion. When she licks the tip of my brother's cock, swirling around the tip, flicking her tongue on the sensitive underside, then sinking down to suck him deep, my knees feel weak. Kain raises his arms, gripping the bars of his metal headboard, staring down at our beautiful girl as she takes care of him in the most pleasurable way and I'm filled with a swell of the most amazing love from my brothers and the woman who has always been our number one girl, even when she had pigtails and scabby knees.

And for the first time in my life, I can see our futures

laid out, ready for us to seize.

EPILOGUE

One month later

DALTON

"I swear, we need to find a new location for the next party," Blake yells over the pounding music at the Red Devil. It wasn't my first choice, but we know the manager and it was easy to arrange.

I'm not one for organizing parties, anyway. If I had my way, my good news would have been marked with dinner at a nice restaurant and an evening spent in bed with Gabriella. It was Gab who insisted that my acceptance into culinary school should be marked by a drunken night out. This is where our age gap starts to show a little!

"There won't be a next party," I yell back. He grins, and rubs his neck, the site of his newest tattoo. I swear, if he doesn't draw a line soon, he'll have no virgin skin left.

"You need another drink," Gabriella slurs, dragging me by the hand to the bar and ordering a complicated number of drink varieties for our friends and family. I'm not sure how she remembers everything under the influence of four Red Devil cocktails, but my girl has skills.

"Are you trying to get me drunk?"

She pats my arm. "Come on, big boy. It's time to

loosen up. You deserve it."

"I still have work tomorrow. This course doesn't start for months and Dad's expecting me to pull my weight until then."

"Your dad can make an exception for tomorrow. In fact, I'm going to message him and tell him you'll be in at midday."

She pulls out her phone and begins to tap away a long message to my dad. I don't bother stopping her because she's the only one Dad will listen to. For whatever reason, he's Gabriella's number one fan. When we finally told him about our relationship, he was happy. I have a feeling it's because Mom used to love Gab so much. She always called her the daughter she never had. Now Dad's going to have her as a daughter-in-law. At least, he will one day. I've already discussed it with my brothers, but we've agreed to wait until Gab has graduated. She doesn't need to be planning for a future when she should be reveling in the present.

Out of the corner of my eye, I spot Celine wobbling on her feet. Since Gabriella's birthday, she's been a liability. Getting drunk, although never bad enough to require a repeat of the hospital treatment, and getting into sticky situations with strangers so that her friends have to drag her out of bars to keep her safe. "Celine's looking like it might be time to send her home in a cab," I tell Gab.

"Are you serious?" She groans, hunting for her friend and shaking her head when she witnesses the unstable dancing that is happening a few feet from us. "What am I going to do with her?"

"She needs a harem," I say, my eyes drifting over my brothers, and Ellie and her triplets. Since we committed to Gabriella, everything about our lives has relaxed. Celine needs that stability. She needs an anchor that can hold her and make her feel safe, even if she doesn't know it.

Maybe that's one guy, but now I'm in my own multiple

love situation, the option of more doesn't seem wild to me anymore.

"I wish she'd start looking at the decent guys who are right in front of her," Gab says. Her eyes linger on Dornan, her friend, who is single and ready to mingle. Then on Travis, who recently quit his job in Germany. There are other decent guys here tonight, men who I'd be happy to date my sister, if I had one.

"Maybe we need to matchmake," I say. "You know, nudge her in the right direction."

"Yeah, but who's going to want that?" she says, grimacing as Celine trips over her own feet and stumbles into a table.

"Someone who sees past her current issues. Someone who knows her well."

Gab folds her arms across her chest, squashing her perfect tits so they rise up, tempting me. I moisten my lips, ready to leave this stupid party so I can get my hands all over this perfect woman who's mine to play with, mine to ravish, and mine to love. But I know she won't leave until her friends do.

Celine stumbles again and this time, Elias is there to catch her. He hefts her up in his huge linebacker arms and strides towards the nearest booth like a lumberjack lugging a log. Her hands swat at his back but they don't seem to bother him in the slightest. A man who's used to demolishing two-hundred-and-fifty-pound opponents isn't going to be fazed by a tiny, incapacitated woman. Gabriella laughs, relieved, and we watch with fascination as he dumps Celine into the booth, practically tossing her onto Travis's lap in his haste.

Celine is a flailing tangle of arms and legs, but she rights herself, gazing around as though she's in a dream. Then she leans toward Travis, her lips banging into his, her arm reflexively hooking around his neck.

My buddy is taken off guard, surprised at the sudden onslaught of woman joined to his face, but despite her drunkenness, Celine must be a good kisser because suddenly, he's responding passionately, while she paws at him.

Damn.

"Seriously!" Gab throws her arms up. "What the fuck is my brother doing?"

"Kissing your friend…they really should get a room," I laugh, but that changes when Elias puts his hand on Celine's shoulder and pulls her away. Her mouth is swollen and glistening, her eyes half shut. "Come on, Celine. You don't need to be doing that…"

His words are cut off by Celine's mouth and her greedy hands which search his body like airport security. Jeez. This is about to get messy. Except, Elias kisses her back too, and Travis looks on, shaking his head, a wry smile on his face.

"Celine's a mess," Dornan says, stepping in beside Gabriella, watching tiny Celine climb Elias like a tree.

"I think you should go rescue Elias," Gab says, nudging Dornan in the direction of the booth. Surprisingly, he listens, and steps in to tap Celine on the shoulder, distracting her enough to stop the kiss.

"Hey, Celine," he says, but doesn't get to finish the sentence because she's already off Elias's lap and latching herself onto Dornan's face. My god, this is going to end in a scuffle. Or Celine being packed off before she can seduce anyone else.

The latter is what happens. Ellie puts her hands between Dornan and Celine, prizing them apart. "Come on, you guys," she says. "Pack it in."

Dornan blinks like he's emerging from a dark tunnel into the midday sunshine and Celine sways, smiling like the cat who got the cream.

"What's wrong, Ellie? I'm just gathering my own harem!"

"I don't think that's how it works, sweetie." Ellie pats her softly on the shoulder.

"I guess it could work that way," I whisper into Gabriella's ear and she shakes her head, rolling her eyes.

"You seriously think that Dornan, Elias, and Travis would share Celine? I mean, you guys are brothers, and Colby, Seb, and Micky are triplets. You were all closely bonded before me and Ellie came along. Travis, Dornan, and Elias barely know each other. In fact, Dornan and Elias have always rubbed each other up the wrong way. It's hardly going to be a match made in heaven."

"I guess," I say, "but stranger things have happened!"

"You're just looking to sprinkle your happiness all over other people. I swear since you started cooking, you've become a big softy."

"Hey!" I put my arm out, flexing my bicep. "I'm still a tough guy," I remind her. "I can still toss you over my shoulder and carry you back to my lair!"

She nods, moistening her lips, her gaze stroking over me hungrily. "Never stop doing that, baby. Never stop."

Ellie takes Celine to a booth with fewer men, and I slide in next to Travis. "Celine, hey?" I wiggle my eyebrows, hoping that he's going to be in a better mood tonight.

"She's trouble," he says. "Looking for love but pretending she just wants sex."

"So like me, Kain, Blake, and Gab then?"

"You knew you wanted love. You just settled for the sex because that's what was offered." Travis really knows how to cut through the bullshit.

"And what about you?" I ask. "Are you looking for love?"

"Nah," he says. "Love is too complicated when nothing else in your life is sorted."

"Maybe just sex then?"

"You're not my type," he grins, and I punch him gently on the shoulder.

"So, when are you planning to make an honest woman of my sister?" he asks, shoving the conversation back into my court.

"You know when. As soon as she graduates."

"You know you have to come to me to ask for my permission?" Travis takes a swig of his beer, smiling at the thought of us groveling to him. I'd crawl on my belly in the dust if it meant I could marry Gabriella and make her mine.

"I have no problem with that, and neither will my brothers."

"I might say yes," he says. "On one condition."

"Oh yeah, and what's that?"

"I get to be your best man."

"There isn't anyone else," I say. "There isn't anyone else."

BLAKE

"I can't believe you booked this place," Kain grumbles, signaling to turn into the parking lot.

"What? Molly's Motel not good enough for you?" I ask.

"It's not good enough for Gabriella," he says.

"Hey, if it was good enough for Ellie, then it's fine for me too. Anyway, I'm not planning to spend much time assessing the decor. Not when I've got three handsome men to keep me busy," Gab says.

"We're going to keep you busy, Gab. Don't you worry about that." Dalton throws his arm around her shoulder in the back seat of the car. She cups his cock through his jeans, and I groan, regretting my stupid seating choice. Then again, Dalton's going to have to get out of this vehicle and nurse a monster erection while we're getting our key card. That'll be fun to watch play out.

As it turns out, my older brother has iron control over his cock and we secure our key card from a receptionist who eyes us suspiciously, obviously questioning the truth of our family reunion story. They probably hear that kind of bullshit all the time.

In the room, Gabriella makes good on her promise. I don't even register the color of the walls before she kisses me, her hands roaming under my shirt. Dalton approaches behind her, cupping Gab's breasts, tugging the hem of her dress up so quickly. We separate our lips with an audible pop so he can tear it over her head. We are a frenzy of hands and lips. Thank goodness for Kain, who takes his time, locking the door, pulling the drapes, and resting the key card on the bedside table. The man is a machine of control and organization.

"Get your fine ass over here," Gab calls out to Kain, stepping out from between me and Dalton to kiss him passionately. He's fully recovered from his injury, the bruises fading within three weeks, but there's still a carefulness about my brother that wasn't there before. I wonder if that will ever leave him or if he'll always be more conscious of the fragility of life. Gab draws back from Kain, looking up into his serious blue gaze. "I want it fast, and after, when we go for round two, we can take our time."

"Yes, ma'am," Kain says, smiling at our bossy girl who isn't afraid to tell us what she needs, confident in the knowledge that we'll deliver.

There's no preamble to what comes next. No slow licking or sucking, no tentative touches, just a hunger that rages and spills, tearing us apart and bringing us together. Tonight, Gab crouches over Dalton's cock, lowering herself onto it and moving just long enough to have him clutching at her thighs before she rises, presenting her perfect ass to a waiting Kain who's kneeling behind, allowing him to take a turn.

Watching the give-and-take is fucking horny, and I stroke my cock in time to their thrusts. When she's driven both my brothers to distraction, I peel her from Dalton's chest and roll her onto her back. She's on birth control now, so neither of my brothers used a condom. As her legs flop open, their cum leaks from inside her and a primal urge to mark her too rises inside me. When I climb over her, I leave my cock to slide over her clit, knowing the metal bar will hit the spot. She groans, grabbing at my shoulder, two orgasms down, and she still wants more.

"Fuck me, Blake. Let me feel your cock."

When I push in deep, my glutes clench, and my toes curl at the perfection of her hot, tight, very wet pussy.

"That's it," she murmurs, eyes rolling back in her head. "That's it."

And it is. It's everything.

Gabriella Cross has always been my perfect fantasy, and now she's my girl, I can't seem to get enough of her. And I think it's because when I look at her, I can see our future, laid out like the patchwork quilt my momma made, all our lives woven together. I can imagine our children; little boys like me, Kain, Dalton, and Travis. Little girls like Gabriella. I can envision us growing and changing together because that's what we've always done. Our path has already led us through so many years of love, laughter, and challenges, and brought us out the other side in one piece. One day, we'll all be sitting on our deck, drinking beer, and soaking up the sunshine, our grandkids at our feet, and that knowledge grounds me in a way I've never felt before.

We reach the pinnacle of pleasure together, wrapped tightly in each other's arms, my brothers by our sides, and after, I kiss her angel tattoo, the permanent reminder of how I'll always see the girl I love.

KAIN

I'm the first to wake, as a shard of light breaks through the unevenly hung drapes and rests over my face. I turn, finding Gabriella nestled against Dalton's chest and Blake fast asleep on his front.

It's still strange for me to see my brothers sleeping. I was used to it when we were kids because we used to camp out, and because, as the youngest, I always seemed to be up first and tapping them awake to play with me.

Now, I have to get used to all of us being together all the time. It's not a hardship because the love between us is strong, but I'm a person who likes his own company, and for things to be organized, and Blake and Dalton aren't like that. I slide off the bed, padding across the linoleum to the bathroom, kicking Blake's jeans and Dalton's shirt out of my path.

Even after we fucked ourselves into dehydration last night, I've still woken with morning wood. Poor Gabriella. I don't think she can take any more. We need to remember that her body has limitations and that we're expecting her to give three times what most other women have to deal with. I stare into the mirror, grateful to see that my face is back to normal. The hollowed eyes I had when I left the hospital have gone, and so has the bruise on my chest. I rest my hand over my heart, its familiar beat reassuring in a way it never was before.

My stomach rumbles and I decide to head out to grab

breakfast before I take a shower. The running water and squeaky pipes in this place will probably wake the whole building.

It's a short walk to the local diner and I pick up breakfast sandwiches, pancakes with berries, and four protein smoothies.

By the time I'm back, Dalton is in the shower and Blake and Gab are sitting up in bed, watching reruns of Friends on the ancient television.

Gab jumps up as soon as she sees me, with no consciousness of how naked she is. With her golden hair tumbling over her body, she's like a mermaid who gave up her tail for a life on the land. A life with her three princes.

"You bought food," she says, taking the large paper bag from my hands. I'm rendered mute by the sight of her pretty breasts and the sweet angel tattoo that's next to her even sweeter pussy. Damn, I think she's trying to kill me.

"I've got something you can eat over here," Blake says, cupping his dick, and I'm jolted from my delicious observations.

"Seriously, dude. Do you have to bring up your cock while I'm thinking about breakfast?"

"I don't think you want me to eat it, baby," Gabriella says with a smile and an arched brow. "But I can suck it after I've had my smoothie."

"See," Blake says, throwing up his arms in victory. "Gab doesn't mind me talking about breakfast dick."

"Please don't call it breakfast dick." I swear, my brothers are going to be the death of me one day!

Gab sucks hard on the straw of her smoothie, hollowing out her cheeks as she stares right at me. "Don't worry, baby," she says, licking her lips. "I love your breakfast dick too."

And suddenly, all my grumpiness slips away. Gabriella somehow knows exactly what to do to disarm me, and I laugh, tossing my head back, pulling her in for a cuddle that starts chastely but turns heated in seconds. I may have excellent self-control, but Gabriella's body pressed against mine unravels all my restraint.

I feed her mouthfuls of pancakes while she sits between my legs, naked and delicious, and after, I trickle golden syrup between her thighs and make a meal all of my own.

And she makes good on her promise to make breakfast dick of all of us, one after another.

GABRIELLA

I've got an assignment to finish, but I don't want to leave this motel room.

It's been a place of epic sex, delicious food, belly twinging laughter, and companionship that makes my heart feel as swollen as an overripe mango.

Blake worked out a way to stream an eighties movie I've been desperate to watch, and Dalton ran out for popcorn and sodas and ended up returning with nachos and candy too. We're all propped up against pillows, laughing at the haircuts and how fashion has made its way around again.

We can only keep focused for fifteen minutes at a time before someone has something funny to say, and Blake pauses it so we can drift off into a hilarious conversation about corn dogs, or Elias's dick getting caught in his jeans. I learn more about the pros and cons of men's underwear than I ever need to know, and it's awesome because it makes me realize just how easy it is for us to be together.

Relationships aren't supposed to be this simple. Even between one man and one woman, they have a fifty percent chance of ending in divorce, or maybe it's even more. But with my amazing Nowak brothers, we never argue. In fact, except for a little lighthearted bickering, I've never seen the brothers argue amongst themselves. I've stumbled into a blissfully simple multiple partner relationship without even trying.

In fact, it was them who almost stumbled headfirst into my vagina! I never thought my vibrator would be the reason I found love, but there you go. Life isn't predictable, and that's what makes it so amazing.

"We're going to have to leave soon," Blake says. "Or we'll go past checkout time."

"I'd happily pay for another night," Kain says, who's met with a flying pillow to the head.

"Can't believe you," Blake grumbles. "After all that moaning yesterday, you want to spend another night wrapped in these nylon sheets?"

"What can I say?" Kain laughs. "Anywhere Gabriella is, I'm happy to be."

"Awww…" I pat his chest affectionately, already working through if I could get my assignment done in a few hours before class. Another night of bliss with my men sounds just about perfect.

"I think we should stay," I say. "Watch another movie. Eat a little more. Fuck away all the calories. Sleep."

Blake, Dalton, and Kain all nod, trying not to smile too broadly because I know they're thinking how perfect that sounds and wondering how they got so lucky. I know because that's exactly what I'm thinking, too.

"You guys ever think about the reason we got together? Because of my brother's perverted stash?" I say.

"I try not to," Kain admits. "I still have his porn collection at the bottom of my closet, and after leafing through one of the mags, I can tell you I won't be looking again."

"Really," I snort. "What was in there?"

"I'll take it to my grave," Kain says, covering his eyes, and we all dissolve into the kind of laughter that warms my heart and fills my soul.

This might have started out as a dial-a-dick deal, but it's ended up in the best kind of forever love. And I couldn't be happier!

ABOUT THE AUTHOR

International bestselling author Stephanie Brother writes high heat love stories with a hint of the forbidden. Since 2015, she's been bringing to life handsome, flawed heroes who know how to treat their women. If you enjoy stories involving multiple lovers, including twins, triplets, stepbrothers, and their friends, you're in the right place. When it comes to books and men, Stephanie truly believes it's the more, the merrier.

She spends most of her day typing, drinking coffee, and interacting with readers.

Her books have been translated into German, French, and Spanish, and she has hit the Amazon bestseller list in seven countries.

Printed in Dunstable, United Kingdom

64276869R00139